Nightmare
in
Morocco

Nightmare in Morocco

Loretta Jackson
and
Vickie Britton

Thorndike Press • Chivers Press
Waterville, Maine USA   Bath, England

This Large Print edition is published by Thorndike Press, USA and by Chivers Press, England.

Published in 2002 in the U.S. by arrangement with Vickie Britton and Loretta Jackson.

Published in 2002 in the U.K. by arrangement with the authors.

U.S. Hardcover 0-7862-4084-9 (Candlelight Series)
U.K. Hardcover 0-7540-4969-8 (Chivers Large Print)

The text of this Large Print edition is unabridged.
Other aspects of the book may vary from the original edition.

Cover design by Thorndike Press Staff.

Set in 16 pt. Plantin by Elena Picard.

Printed in the United States on permanent paper.

British Library Cataloguing-in-Publication Data available

Library of Congress Cataloging-in-Publication Data

Jackson, Loretta.
   Nightmare in Morocco / Loretta Jackson and
Vickie Britton.
     p. cm.
   ISBN 0-7862-4084-9 (lg. print : hc : alk. paper)
   1. Tour guides (Persons) — Fiction. 2. Morocco —
Fiction. 3. Large type books. I. Britton, Vickie. II. Title.
PS3560.A224 N54 2002
   813′.54—dc21   2002018021

To friend and mentor,
Leon Woods

Chapter One

As she looked across the deep blue water of the Mediterranean toward Tangier, Noa Parker felt the familiar shiver of fear Morocco always caused in her. From the ferry she watched the sloping hillside, packed with square blocks of buildings, gleam white in the brilliant sun.

From this distance Noa could not glimpse the thick, ancient walls of the medina — the old town — behind which tiny, open-fronted shops lined each side of narrow passageways that wound in intricate, endless mazes. Yet the medina seemed once again to enclose her, as it had when, as a child of eight, she had become separated from her father and had fled for hours in those terrifying passageways, intensely frightened, hopelessly lost.

Noa leaned out over the railing, trying to spot the silver car lettered *Carlson-Rand Tours*. She knew why her boss, Wendell

Carlson, had insisted on meeting her himself at the ferry landing: He wanted her to guide his new tour, which was to venture deep into the heart of Morocco. Noa straightened her shoulders determinedly. She was satisfied with the schedule she had kept for the past five summers, managing in-depth tours of Spain and Portugal, countries she knew well. Mr. Carlson could be very persuasive, but Noa intended to remain firm in her decision not to include Morocco in her itinerary.

With a sort of panic she thought again of the medina. She recalled how darkness had started to fall upon the shadowy shops hung with woven rugs, blankets, and brass items. The crowd of tourists had thinned, leaving turbaned peddlers whose dark, unapproachable faces and strange, hooded figures made them seem like medieval monks terrifyingly slow of step. Noa would never forget the foreign cries of street vendors intermingled with the pleas of a blind beggar tapping his cane in front of him.

Noa's father had enlisted boys on donkeys to find her. When they had succeeded, many hours later, Dad had tried to distract her by setting her astride one of the straggly animals. Noa had sat sobbing upon the donkey until they had reached the hotel. Strangely enough, seventeen years later she could still feel the terror.

"In just an hour," the woman beside her said, "you can go from Christian Europe to Moslem Africa — into another world. It doesn't seem possible." She drew closer to Noa and gripped the railing tautly. Noa saw her hands before seeing her face — strong, work-hardened hands free of the polish and jewelry that characterized those of the tourists, hands that spoke of strength and independence.

The woman's face had the same qualities, though her words had sounded dry and stilted rather than enthusiastic, as if she were accustomed to making forced comments.

Because Noa's maroon jacket bore the insignia *Carlson-Rand Tours* in black-on-gold letters, she was used to having strangers approach her. She loved their excited remarks and never tired of their questions. This woman was obviously not a tourist. "Are you from Spain?" Noa asked her.

"I'm Marie Landos. I was born in California, but I work in Madrid."

"I'm Noa Parker."

"I know Wendell Carlson," Marie volunteered, eyes falling to the insignia Noa wore. Her voice, like her face, had a tinge of hardness. Rigid, clipped curls, tinted a dark yellow, gave her an air of artificiality. She was probably in her late fifties. Her eyes were the same color as the ice-blue Mediterranean and, Noa thought, were just as cold.

"Do you know this hotel?" Marie asked, showing her a slip of paper.

Noa glanced at the paper, which gave the address of the Hotel Maroc. "Yes. If you catch the local bus at the ferry station, this hotel will be your first stop. It's the tall white building on the corner. Very elegant. You can't miss it."

"So here we are," Marie said. "Enjoy Morocco."

Enjoy Morocco — something Noa couldn't do. She and Marie started down the long plank together, but became separated in the jostling crowd. Noa soon forgot their brief conversation in trying to locate her trim, aristocratic boss. Turning down Wendell Carlson's offer wasn't going to be easy. Besides being the owner of the tour company that paid her generously, he had been a lifelong friend of Noa's late father. She must take great care to decline his offer with some semblance of grace.

As Noa stopped to scan the crowd, she noticed a tall, lean man watching her. His face, sharp and dark, caused Noa to think

10

again of the medina, in spite of the fact that he wore a white business suit like those the British often wear in warm climates, and he had about him that same assured air.

His handsome face lit in a smile of recognition as he strode toward her. "Noa Parker?"

Standing very close to her now, he looked even more Arabian, making her think of slender white horses and desert sand. About him was a scent of tangy spice. His dark eyes gazed deeply into hers as he said in perfect English, "Wendell Carlson can't meet you. He sent me instead. I'm Taber Rand." He took her arm and began guiding her through the swarm of people, saying as he did, "I wouldn't have known you without the insignia. Mr. Carlson didn't mention your tawny hair. And the name Noa is misleading," he said with a smile. "I guess I expected an old man with a long, white beard or someone carrying a dictionary."

"And I didn't expect Rand instead of Carlson. Are you related to Thomas Rand?"

"I'm his son."

The reply made Noa instinctively wary. All Noa really remembered about Thomas Rand was his strong British accent and bad temper, but she had suspected him of fraud and deception.

"It was a mistake from the very start, letting Thomas Rand into the business," Wendell Carlson had once confided in Noa several years ago, just after the two partners had fallen out. Mr. Carlson had bought Rand's half of the company and had never spoken of him or to him again. But for some reason that still puzzled her, Wendell Carlson had left the Rand name on the tour. Once more Noa wondered why, and what now possessed Mr. Carlson to hire Thomas Rand's son.

"You expected me to look like Father." Taber's smile revealed very white, even teeth. "Everyone does. But my mother was Moroccan." He opened the door to the tour car. "It's my duty to talk you into committing yourself to this tour. It's very important to Mr. Carlson. He won't hear of another guide."

"I could give you my answer right now," Noa said.

Taber laughed. "Give me a chance, Noa. Over lunch."

"I had lunch on the ferry," Noa told him after they had parked and were walking along a street whose noisy medievalism was such a contrast to the stately quietness of Spain. Her thoughts echoed Marie's words on the ferry — this was another world!

12

Noise encircled them: a hammering and banging of craftsmen, the cries of street traders, a call of "Balak" from a man on a donkey.

Noa hurried slightly ahead of Taber Rand. The faces of the hooded people sitting on the ground in the midst of carts of vegetables and squawking chickens made her more and more uneasy.

"Wait," Taber said, catching up with her and smiling at her discomfort. "In Morocco we never rush. It's considered undignified."

Noa slowed her pace to his. She felt comforted by his closeness.

A raggedy-looking boy started following them. He slid two thick silver bracelets from the collection on his arm and jangled them before Noa, saying in English, "You buy?"

Before she could reply, Taber spoke for her. "She doesn't have money to buy anything," he said.

Discouraged by Taber's definite tone, the boy scurried away.

"In Morocco the husband's word is still law," Taber explained with an arresting smile. "I often rescue women tourists from the street hawkers by posing as their spouse."

"I don't know if I like being taken for one of your wives." The incident reminded Noa that Morocco was a distinctly different culture, where women's rights were still only a dream of the future.

"Would you rather own a stack of cheap jewelry?" Taber quipped. "The street peddlers can be very persistent, especially with pretty young American women."

"Since you put it that way, thank you — I guess."

From the busy roadway they turned into a cobbled path shaded by a thatched roof. The path led through a sunken garden whose lush green plants were a pleasant surprise after the hot, dusty street. Ahead of her now, Taber went through an archway into a large room braced by slender columns and tiled with spirals of tiny green-and-brown mosaics.

Taber waited for her in the center of the room, his strong, alert features dark against the white of his clothing. Noa was both flattered and disquieted by the way his glowing black eyes gazed into hers, as if there were nothing else in the room, or in the world, except her. He indicated a secluded table and sat down opposite her.

He spoke in French to a waiter wearing a long, flowing garment and a Turkish-style fez, and the man leisurely brought them tea. Noa's busy morning and her plan to decline

Carlson-Rand's offer began to recede in her mind as she became immersed in the restaurant's exotically Moorish atmosphere.

Taber's dark eyes continued to watch her as she sipped the tea. The sweet, warm liquid, fragrant with mint, relaxed her.

"It's not Rick's Café," Taber said, referring to the nightclub in the Humphrey Bogart movie *Casablanca*, "but it *is* mine. I bought this place last year, my personal retreat from the world."

"It's very beautiful."

"My home is only a short distance from here." He leaned closer. "This is my first assignment as tour manager. That's why I must convince you to guide this tour. The success of this Moroccan venture is very important to Mr. Carlson — and to me. No one likes to begin a job by failing."

He looked as if he had never failed at anything. "You have at least fifty guides to choose from. Why me?"

"Because Wendell Carlson wants the very best. He says that's you."

"I'm afraid —"

Taber's lean hand covered hers for an instant, sending a tingle of excitement through Noa. His smile showed white, even teeth. "Rule number one: Don't be afraid."

"I've always worked in Spain and Portugal. I don't know that much about Morocco."

"Noa, I'll make a deal with you. You take this assignment, and I'll go along with you on the first tour. It will give me a chance to straighten out the problems that are bound to arise with a new venture. I'll take full responsibility and still give you full pay." The dark eyes were so persuasive. "How can you refuse?"

"I have reasons. Personal ones."

Taber drank some tea as if he had accepted her answer as final. No doubt that would mean she would never see him again. She felt vaguely disappointed.

A woman seated on a stool at the bar now turned. Noa recognized her as Marie Landos, the woman she had talked to on the ferry. Surprised, Noa waved to her.

Marie stood up quickly, straightening the long, oatmeal-colored suit that hung loosely on her thin, angular body, and headed toward their table.

Noa caught the exchange of glances between Taber and Marie. Noa was puzzled at the change that came over him. His friendly, rather ironic tone became coldly formal. "Marie," he said, rising. "What brings you to Tangier?"

"We meet again," the woman said to Noa,

then answered Taber, "Business. What else does one have at my age?"

"Won't you join us?"

"No. No, I just dropped by to see if Wendell was here. Whenever I'm in the neighborhood, I look for him. It seems I've chased him over continents." She gave a brief, brittle laugh and said to Noa, "Elusive men are so charming."

"He's still in London. Is there something I can help you with?"

"Nothing, Taber. I heard he's starting a tour through here. I might book it for the girls at St. Theresa's. Anyway, tell Wendell I'll catch him on the next trip."

Taber seemed relieved as she made her quick exit. "Marie teaches travel-study classes at an exclusive girls' school in Madrid. She's a real cosmopolitan, from the old school, with the same problem all you Americans have — excessive speed."

Taber unfolded a brochure from his pocket. Smoothing the yellow map, he said, "Fez, Rabat, Casablanca, Marrakesh. Have you ever been to Marrakesh? It's exciting! The Sahara Desert begins just beyond." Pointing on the map to a spot near Marrakesh, he said, "Here's where I had planned to teach you to ride a camel. You'll never get such an opportunity again."

17

Noa smiled at the thought of their riding together through the desert — Noa and her sheik. Wouldn't it be fun touring with him, learning from him? She thought of the long, lonely years during her father's final illness, when all thoughts of freedom and romance had been suppressed. She suddenly wanted very much to accept this offer. Nothing was keeping her from it except a silly, childish fear she should have long ago put aside.

Taber seemed to pick up on her thoughts. "Because my mother was a native of Morocco, I have Morocco in my heart," he said, hitting his hand against his chest. "I could teach you about these people, who are one-half mine. With knowledge, you will find acceptance," he said, "and acceptance is the key!"

Noa still had qualms, but she asked hesitantly, "When does the tour begin?"

"One month and three days from now, right here in Tangier."

Should she change her mind because she was drawn to him? Her heartbeat quickened as she gazed into his eyes.

"Please, Noa, say you'll be our first guide! Work this tour with me."

Noa felt a little mesmerized by the smoldering, dark eyes that refused to be rejected. Their hypnotic force seemed to draw from her the words she felt she shouldn't speak: "All right, I'll sign up for just this tour. After that, I make no promises."

On the ferry heading back to Spain, Noa wondered what had caused her sudden change of mind, when even her long friendship with Wendell Carlson could not have accomplished it. She sat on one of the deck chairs and watched the white-capped waves and the receding shoreline. A month seemed like such a very long time. Remembering Taber's face, she felt a return of her fascination. She had not experienced such an instant attraction for anyone before. She knew she had accepted this tour only because she wanted to see Taber Rand again!

Upon Noa's arrival at her estate in Algeciras, a telegram awaited her. Its very presence seemed a harbinger of bad news, and she hastily put the rest of her mail aside to read it.

Frightened by its cold brevity, she read and reread the urgent message: *Mike's ill. Come quickly.* No doubt her brother's adopted daughter, Cathy, had sent the telegram, but it had no signature.

With trembling fingers, she put a call through to Cathy. Their conversation confirmed what she had feared the most: Mike had suffered a second heart attack a few days ago. He had been taken to Memorial South, where he was still in intensive care.

Noa was relieved she had nothing scheduled before the Moroccan tour, making it possible for her to make immediate preparations to leave for New York. If only she could be there immediately! The eight-hour flight would give her too much time to think, too many hours to sit, alone and afraid.

Noa and her older brother were very close. Since their father's death two years ago, his calls and letters had come with faithful regularity. She knew that Mike had never quite recovered from that last heart attack in May, but of course he had refused to slow down. Now, something about talking to Cathy on the phone sounded tragically final. Noa tried to prepare herself for what she was certain awaited her. Tears filled her eyes. Mike! What would she ever do without him?

The long, dismal hours of flight gave no answer. From talking to Cathy on the phone, Noa had received the impression that the girl would meet her at Kennedy Airport, but no one was waiting. Noa stayed for a while in the terminal, then lingered outside, where a damp wind whipped at her hair and clothing. She decided she should have known better. Cathy had never liked her. And deep in Noa's heart, although she pretended otherwise, she had never liked or accepted Cathy. Perhaps Mike had spoiled Cathy because he was trying to make up for the fact that she was adopted, for the fact that his wife had died in an accident when the girl was only three. Cathy was the source of Mike's many unhappy letters proclaiming the trials of the single parent.

In spite of exhaustion and jet lag, Noa took a cab directly to Memorial South. At the entrance to the intensive-care unit, a nurse rose at her inquiry. "Are you Mr. Parker's sister?" she asked somberly.

Noa's heart pounded. "Yes. May I see him?"

The stout nurse came around the desk and took her arm. "My dear . . ." she said. The deep silence that followed told Noa that what she feared had indeed happened. Mike was dead!

"The heart attack was very severe," the nurse began to explain, stopping at the sight of Noa's tears. All Noa could think about was that sometime during the endless flight between Algeciras and New York, Mike had died without ever seeing her again.

Through her grief, Noa suddenly thought

of Cathy. "Is Mike's daughter here?" she asked the nurse.

"She took a cab home about half an hour ago. Just after Mr. Parker . . . passed away."

Numb with shock, Noa began to move away. She could barely feel the nurse's arm gently guiding her to a nearby room. "Wait here," the nurse said. "Mr. Parker left something for you."

Several people waited in the small room, turning pages of magazines as if they did not notice her sobbing. It wasn't fair that she would never see Mike again! It wasn't fair that her brother had died so young! Even separated by an ocean, she and Mike had always depended on each other. Mike was the last of her family. Now she had no one left in the world!

The nurse handed her a folded paper, saying, "He made me promise to give this directly to you and not to the girl. He dictated the words, and I wrote them down for you shortly after he was admitted. It was as if he knew. . . ."

Noa sat for a while, the unread note in her hands. Only yesterday, feeling a promise of joy, Noa had left Taber and Morocco. Now her world had crumbled. How could things change with such cruel rapidity?

Some time later Noa unfolded the paper

and read Mike's words, written in the nurse's dainty, unfamiliar handwriting:

Noa,

I know you never break your word! Promise me you will take Cathy back with you to Spain. She has fallen in with bad company. She is dating the devil himself! You must get her away from his influence! Do this for me, Noa. I love her very much. She has just turned seventeen. I know a year will make a lot of difference. I love you and I know I can count on you to watch her for me.

Mike

Her vision blurred by her tears and by hours of sleeplessness, Noa read and reread the note. She was only seven years older than Cathy. How could she keep such a promise? From what she knew about Cathy, how could anyone?

Noa gave the taxi driver the Oak Terrace address and watched the streets grow hilly, narrow, and more residential. Thin, mistlike rain had begun, dampening her face and hair. She paid the driver and walked toward the white, impersonal building in which Mike had shared a condominium with Cathy.

23

Passing a series of doors that all looked alike, she found the one marked *Mike Parker.* "It's open!" The voice that acknowledged her knock could barely be heard above the clamor of hard rock music.

Noa opened the door. Cathy sat drinking a bottle of pop. Topped with a careless mass of brown hair, her head had a defiant set to it, one she had carried even as a child. The defiance even showed itself in the slow way she continued drinking, in the way her eyes remained locked on Noa over the tilted bottle.

Noa set her suitcase near the stereo and turned down the volume. "I've just come from the hospital."

The girl had fresh, clear skin and large, indefinite-colored eyes that now were a pale brown flecked with yellow. They stared at Noa without any emotion. Mike had built his entire life around Cathy. Didn't she even care that he was gone?

Noa's throat began aching with a resentment she must not allow to show. "I can't believe it," she said, and sank down into a chair.

Quietness surrounded them, and in her grief Noa momentarily forgot Cathy was present. The girl's voice called her back.

"Mike told me I had to go back to Spain

with you," Cathy said, tipping the bottle to her lips again. "What if I don't want to?"

What if I don't want you to? Noa thought angrily but did not say. In the silence she felt an intense dislike for Cathy. At last, a little ashamed of her hostility, she said, "We'll talk about it in the morning."

"Good. I've got a date tonight."

"You surely aren't going out tonight? Mike's just . . . I must insist that you stay home tonight. Your date will have to wait."

Noa had expected Cathy to challenge her, but the strange, yellowish eyes remained indifferent.

"Who were you going out with?"

Cathy spoke slowly, affectedly. "Mike always minded his own business. Why don't you?"

Trying to ignore her last remark, Noa asked, "Don't you call him Father?"

"He wasn't my father."

No use even attempting to talk to her, Noa thought. She must not let her pain get them off to a bad start. Trying not to sound impatient, Noa said calmly, "The flight over was terrible. I've got such a headache that I'm going to have to rest. Where should I sleep?"

Cathy shrugged. "You can sleep in Mike's bed. Or on the sofa."

Noa found a blanket in the closet and stretched out on the couch. Stiff and cramped from the long hours in flight, her body found no position comfortable. She forced herself to lie still, an arm across her face to block the glare of the overhead light.

Noa closed her eyes, wishing she could shut out reality. She was grateful that Cathy made no attempt to talk to her. Despite the bright lights and the music, which Cathy had turned up once again, Noa dozed off.

When she awoke, Cathy was gone.

Chapter Two

Music blared, and the singer's voice could barely be heard above the brass and drumbeat. Cathy had not bothered to decrease the volume, nor had she stopped to switch off the overhead chandelier.

Fitful sleep had given Noa a sense of great physical heaviness, but she forced herself to rise, to check one huge, whitewashed room after another. The sight of Mike's empty bed made her want to cry; so did seeing Cathy's.

How could Cathy do this to her? Angrily Noa switched off the stereo. The thick silence made her aware of how impossible it would be to find Cathy in New York City.

But it was only ten-thirty. Surely the girl had just stepped out momentarily!

The shrilly ringing phone startled her. That must be Cathy now. Relieved, she lifted the receiver.

"Noa?" She recognized at once her boss's

deep, steady voice. "I got your message on my answering machine. How is Mike?"

"Wendell, he's gone!" Her voice broke. "I didn't even get to see him!"

Wendell hesitated, then said with deep sincerity, "Noa, I'm so sorry. I was afraid of that the minute I heard. In fact, I intended to catch a flight out at once, but I can't leave now. I just got out of the hospital, and the doctor has given me a definite no."

"I didn't know you were in the hospital. What's wrong?"

"A little spell with my heart. That's why I didn't meet you in Tangier. Nothing to worry about, though. A person expects a little trouble at my age, but Mike . . . he was just a young man. I can't believe it! I'd give anything to be with you now!"

Noa imagined Wendell Carlson's dignified but weathered face, creased with deep laugh lines. She could see his brown hair, threaded now with gray, limply falling over his forehead, and his eyes, which often appeared to laugh at the world, clouded with intense emotion. Noa tried to drive the disappointment from her voice. "I'll be fine. You just take care of yourself."

"What are your plans?"

"I'll lease the condominium and bring Cathy back with me."

"Good. I'm counting on you to start my Moroccan tour!"

After she hung up, she continued to think about Wendell, how good he had always been to her, how much his call had comforted her. Wendell and her father had been as close as brothers. If Cathy didn't object, she would give him Dad's gold watch, the one that Mike always carried.

When Cathy hadn't appeared by three a.m., Noa began to wonder if she should call the police. She paced around and ended up in the corridor with the brilliant lights, which exaggerated the hall's white emptiness.

Cathy's voice startled her. "Are you looking for me?"

Where had she come from? Certainly not from the outside entrance. "Where have you been?" Noa demanded.

Without a word, Cathy bypassed her into the front room.

"I asked you where you've been."

"Out," Cathy replied with an infuriating mock innocence, as if she had no idea what Noa was talking about. The girl wore jeans and a sloppy sweatshirt, but her eyes were carefully made up with dark mascara that seemed to emphasize the girl's surly defiance.

"I was worried about you."

"Look, I don't like you and you don't like me," Cathy responded angrily. "So don't pretend to be worried about me. I'm not your problem."

She hurried off into the kitchen, snapping on lights.

"That's where you're wrong. I'm your legal guardian until you come of age. That's twelve months from now."

Acting as if she didn't hear her, Cathy took a package of candy bars from the cupboard and began unwrapping one.

"You probably haven't even eaten supper. That's not good for you." As Noa spoke, she found a cup and reached for the coffee beneath the drip coffee maker.

"Neither is coffee," the girl retorted.

"We might just as well get along," Noa said, trying to sound matter-of-fact. "You're going to have to come back with me to Spain."

Cathy munched the candy bar, regarding Noa with cool, impassive dislike. "I'm not leaving New York City."

"This apartment will have to be leased. You won't have any place to stay."

"I have friends." Noa remembered how Mike's letter had referred to the bad company Cathy had been keeping. Cathy's eyes narrowed. "You can't make me go to Spain with you, not if I don't want to go. If I were you, I wouldn't even try."

What had Mike gotten her into? With effort, Noa bit back the bitter words on the tip of her tongue. Daylight was only a few hours away. She had funeral arrangements to make, all of Mike's business to settle. Any showdown between Cathy and her would have to wait.

When Noa saw Mike's lawyer a few days after the funeral, he informed Noa that she was sole beneficiary of Mike's estate. Mike had worked for Intermax, a huge investment firm, and most of his money — a sizeable fortune — had been put into short-term investments.

The aging lawyer cited Cathy's immaturity and emotional problems to explain why she had been totally disinherited, but his extreme reticence gave Noa the impression that he knew much more about her niece than he was willing to reveal.

The vast fortune they were discussing did not pose any problems. Noa knew she could invest it wisely, so both she and Cathy would have a secure future. In fact, she knew exactly how she would invest it: She would buy into Carlson-Rand Tours. She would become Wendell Carlson's partner and fulfill her late father's unrealized dream, a dream that had become hers also.

But being responsible for a wayward, teenage girl who apparently detested her was a very heavy burden. "Why didn't Mike set up a trust fund for her?" she asked the lawyer.

"Perhaps he realized Cathy needs something no amount of money can buy." As if unwilling to discuss the subject further, the lawyer drew a paper from his file. "Here's a list of Mike's valuables, mostly coins."

Even as a boy, Mike had treasured his coins. Then the collection had consisted of a few Indian-head pennies in a tin box under his bed; now the coins, some valued at a thousand dollars each, were worth a substantial sum. "Where does he keep them?"

"You know how Mike wanted them right with him. No doubt they are somewhere in the apartment."

Dread of her new responsibilities deepened as Noa left his office. By the time the huge condominium building came into view, her qualms had changed to real fear. As far as Cathy was concerned, Noa was never going to be able to live up to Mike's expectations of her!

"Why did Mike leave me out?" Cathy demanded after Noa had explained the terms of Mike's will. "I'm his daughter! I can't believe he left me without even a stinking roof over my head!"

"I don't want to talk about the money right now."

"I do!" Cathy trailed Noa into the hallway. "What are you doing, anyway? Why are you snooping around?"

"I'm trying to find some of Mike's valuables. We'll want to put them in a safety-deposit box before we leave."

Cathy sniffed. "I'm not going anywhere!" Still, to Noa's surprise, she began helping to search the rooms.

"I would like to give Dad's watch to Wendell Carlson, if you don't mind."

"Why should you care if I mind? I'm disinherited. I'm nobody!"

But a detailed search uncovered no watch to give anyone, nor could they find the other items of jewelry on the lawyer's list.

"Do you know where Mike kept his coin collection?" Noa asked.

"In here." Noa followed Cathy back into Mike's room. The neatness and order, so distinctly Mike's, saddened her and made her anxious to get the job done.

Cathy pointed to the bed. "He kept them in a box under there."

Inside the huge container were a few silver dollars and a scattering of old nickels, dimes, and quarters. But the rare coins, the ones on the list the lawyer had given her, were not there!

Noa ran her fingers through the coins that remained. They clinked together loudly. "The valuable coins are missing."

Cathy looked away. "Maybe Mike sold them."

Noa felt a sick feeling clutch at her heart. The gold rings could have been lost, the watch easily misplaced. But Mike would never have parted with his coins! What could this mean? She glanced at Cathy, who still stared at the rug. When the girl finally did lift her head, Noa saw what might have been a trace of guilt in her eyes.

Since Mike's funeral, the issue of Cathy's going to Spain with Noa had hung, unresolved, in the air between them. Noa finally decided that when dealing with Cathy, the firm, no-nonsense approach was best. Two tickets to Spain now lay in a neat packet inside Noa's purse. Mike's obstinate daughter was going to get on that plane with her Monday morning, Noa silently vowed, even if she had to carry her, kicking and screaming, all the way.

As the cab approached the condominium building, Noa felt her stomach constrict at the thought of another angry confrontation with Cathy. Over the past few days it seemed she had grown steadily more surly and petulant, more resentful of Noa's intrusion into her life. After leaving the cab, Noa squared her shoulders and took a deep breath, mentally preparing herself for the forthcoming fight. Gathering her courage, she marched directly up to where Cathy, painting her nails a brilliant red, lounged upon the sofa.

"I've bought tickets for our flight to Spain," Noa said in her most authoritative voice, tossing the tickets onto the nearby table for emphasis.

Cathy did not look up from the last painted nail.

"You heard me, didn't you?" Noa demanded. "I said that I've bought tickets to Spain — for both of us!"

Cathy glanced up, no smile on her lips, the yellowish eyes totally expressionless.

"I'm getting pretty tired of your attitude. You *are* going to be on that plane! I'm not going to put up with any of your pouting or arguments!"

Cathy shrugged slightly, as if the matter was of absolutely no importance to her. "So when do we leave?" she asked casually.

Almost too stunned to answer, Noa groped for a reply, her mind still occupied with words of threat and persuasion. "In three days," she finally said.

"That doesn't give me much time to pack."

"It's all we can spare." Wary of a trick, she asked, "What made you decide to come peaceably?"

Cathy shrugged. "I decided I want to see Spain."

"How would you like to see Morocco too?" Noa asked, explaining about the tour scheduled only days after their return to Algeciras. "I'd like to take you along with me."

"Why not?" Cathy replied with the same resigned nonchalance with which she now accepted the trip to Spain. She finished another nail and blew on it. "You will let me buy some new clothes, won't you?"

"It's a promise!" Later Noa might regret her words, but at the moment a new wardrobe seemed an insignificant price to pay for her sullen niece's cooperation. In fact, it seemed a great bargain!

For the first time, she saw Cathy actually smile. She would be an attractive girl if she rid herself of that pout and that perpetual scowl, Noa thought. Noa felt a spark of hope, even enthusiasm. Maybe they would get along after all; perhaps the girl would fill the great void left by Mike.

"I think I'll get my hair done tomorrow," Cathy announced.

"That's a good idea. A good cut will keep you from having to fuss with it on the trip."

"That's not exactly what I meant," Cathy replied, running a hand through the tousled brown waves. "Oh, forget it! What kind of clothes will I need?"

"I'd bring mostly slacks and cool comfortable blouses. And comfortable shoes. The climate is warm, but I wouldn't advise skimpy tops or short shorts. They'll only make you feel conspicuous. Morocco is still a very conservative country. Many of the women still cover their faces with veils."

"No kidding!"

"I could go shopping with you," Noa suggested.

"I don't think so," Cathy said, with a critical glance at Noa's neat cotton skirt and blouse. "Just give me the money." With an exaggerated sweep of her hand, she put the finishing touches on her nails.

When Noa returned to the apartment the following day, her first alarmed impression was that a stranger had slipped in and made herself at home in front of the television set. Another startled glance told her that it was Cathy.

"Hi," Cathy greeted her. Noa avoided looking directly at the stiff, bold streaks of platinum running through the once soft, pretty brown hair. "So what do you think? I had it streaked and tipped. The hairdresser says it looks real European."

"I — I liked it better the way it was," Noa said, recovering her power of speech.

"It was yuk before! This is the real me," Cathy asserted, turning her head this way and that. She was obviously pleased with the mess they had made of her hair. The bold, bleached-blond streaks would make heads turn here in New York City; Noa dreaded the impression Cathy would make in the Moroccan villages, where few light-haired tourists were seen, and where many local women were still quite conservative.

Impulsively Cathy grasped Noa's arm. "Come on. I want you to see my new clothes."

Noa's mouth dropped open at the sight of several pairs of high, spiky heels; a host of skimpy tops and leather miniskirts; a backless cocktail dress; and, to top everything off, a pile of chunky, garish golden bangle bracelets.

"This is . . . all?"

"I could have gotten more if you'd given me more money," Cathy said, an edge of sulkiness creeping into her voice. "At least Mike wasn't stingy."

"I gave you over three hundred dollars! You . . . you didn't buy any tennis shoes?"

Cathy held up a pair of fragile sandals. "I got these instead."

Noa imagined Cathy's mingling with the rest of the tour group with her New Wave hairdo, dressed in a series of wild, impractical outfits. Why, she'd make laughingstocks of them both! In a flush of anger, Noa wondered if that was what Cathy intended.

"These things will have to go back to the stores," Noa said.

"Why?"

"They aren't . . . appropriate. As I tried to explain to you before, Morocco is a very conservative country. Women just don't dress this way."

"I'll dress any way I want!"

"If you make yourself conspicuous, you'll draw unwelcome attention to yourself."

"I don't care! I like my clothes and I like my new hairdo and I'm not going to change the way I look for anyone or anything!"

"I'm afraid you'll regret it," Noa said quietly, but even as she spoke, she realized she herself was far more likely to be sorry.

Noa gripped the railing tightly as the ferry began to dock. "What's wrong?" Cathy asked, observing her curiously from behind lavender sunglasses the exact color of her skintight blouse. "Did you get seasick?"

"No, I'm fine." Noa thought of how ridiculous her fear of returning to Morocco would seem to Cathy, how Cathy would scoff at her sense of dread. To rid herself of the uneasy sensation settling over her like some dire premonition, Noa filled her mind with thoughts of Taber.

She thought of the deep red flowers he'd sent her. She'd discovered them, a little wilted from their long wait, on the doorstep of her small, Spanish-style home in Algeciras. During the few days she and Cathy were there, Noa had nursed them back to health with sunshine and water. Every time she looked at them, she thought of Taber's dark hair and eyes.

The local bus took them to Hotel Tangier, one of the tall, white stucco buildings that overlooked the famous railway and the sea. As soon as they were settled, Cathy disappeared into the hotel gift shop.

Rattan furniture was scattered informally around a huge, brilliantly tiled lobby. Noa looked around for Taber and finally sank down on a couch facing the door so she could watch the assorted passersby in business suits, shorts, or jellabas with drooping hoods.

A young man approached. After tossing a canvas bag onto the chair across from her, he stood reading a pamphlet. He looked fresh, clean, and all-American, like Huck Finn grown up and glad to be on another adventure. His hair, slightly long, was a very light brown, and his eyes kept meeting hers.

"Are you with the Carlson-Rand tour?" he asked, smiling.

"I'm Noa Parker, tour guide."

"Count on me to ask an obvious question." He grinned and added, "The emblem on your blouse matches the one on my flight bag." He stepped closer, extended his hand in a distinctly American way, and said, "Greg Corbin, from New Jersey."

Cathy would like the black net shirt that exaggerated his broad shoulders, but fit tightly around his thin waist and hips. He seated himself beside her. "This is my first time out of the States," he said.

"My niece is from New York," Noa volunteered, recognizing in Greg's voice the same faint, Eastern accent that was in Cathy's. Noa was glad the nice appearing man, somewhere near Cathy's age, was joining the tour. Maybe it would make the trip more interesting for her. Any girl would find him attractive. "She's going to be on the tour too."

"I hope she's as pretty as you," Greg replied.

"There's Cathy now," Noa said, pretending not to notice the admiring eyes still fastened on her. Noa called to Cathy, motioning her over. "Cathy, this is Greg Corbin. He'll be joining us on the tour."

Greg rose and once again extended his hand.

Noa expected Cathy to act giggly and flirtatious; instead she merely mumbled, "Hi," and kept her head down, avoiding the young man's eyes. Noa was puzzled by her behavior; she had never believed Cathy to be shy.

"Can I buy you two ladies cold drinks? We can sit out by the pool."

Noa glanced at Cathy, who seemed unenthusiastic but willing. They passed through an adjoining room and into a pool area with fragile white tables no one was using.

"What kind of mixed drinks do you have?" Cathy asked the waiter.

Intervening before the waiter could answer, Noa said, "We'll both have Cokes," undaunted by the hateful look Cathy shot toward her.

Greg continued to direct his conversation to Noa. Cathy slipped on her sunglasses, sipped her Coke, and ignored both of them.

As soon as Cathy finished her drink, she pulled back her chair. "See ya," she said, sauntering off with what seemed an exaggerated sway of the very tight jeans.

Noa was a little embarrassed by her rudeness, but Greg seemed unoffended. He pulled his chair a little closer. "So would you like to have dinner with me tonight? I hear the food's good here at the hotel."

"Me?" Noa was surprised by his invitation.

Greg grinned. "Why not? You're not married, are you?"

Surprise made Noa look at him closely for the first time. The laugh lines that crinkled about his blue-green eyes told her that he was older than she had first believed, definitely more her age than Cathy's. Noa had been so busy playing matchmaker that she hadn't realized Greg's interest was in her. Perhaps she had unknowingly led him to believe she was interested; if so, she would have to discourage him.

"I'm sorry. There's always so much to do before a new tour." She rose. "In fact, I should be going —"

"I understand," Greg said. "I'll see you

tomorrow, then, at the get-acquainted meeting."

"Eight o'clock sharp," Noa said with a smile.

Noa went back to her room and was studying tomorrow morning's itinerary when the hotel phone rang.

"Noa? This is Taber."

She was relieved and happy to hear his deep voice. "I was beginning to wonder if you were going to show up tonight," she said.

"I've been on the run most of the day. I'm afraid we're starting this tour out with a real catastrophe. Of the twenty-eight people we had scheduled, fifteen have cancelled out."

Noa drew in her breath. "How could that be?"

"Our group of retired teachers ate some tainted chicken at their bon-voyage party. It put most of them in the hospital. They'll recover, but they had to reschedule."

"Are we going to go ahead with the tour?"

"What else can we do?"

"How many does that leave?"

"I hope you're not superstitious, Noa. Excluding the guides and the bus driver, the addition of your niece Cathy makes a group of thirteen."

Noa laughed, but deep inside she felt another tinge of foreboding.

"Listen, Noa, we have so much to discuss. If you haven't eaten yet, why don't you meet me in the dining room?"

"I was going to skip supper."

"I could use some company — and some consolation!"

"Just give me a few minutes to get ready."

Noa hastily changed into a simple blue cotton dress, pinned her long hair up with a silver clip, and went directly to the dining room. Taber rose quickly when he saw her. The deep maroon jacket made his hair and eyes appear brighter, darker. He was even more handsome than she remembered!

Excitement quickened as his warm hand grasped hers. "I hope you like seafood," he said. "I ordered shrimp, the house specialty, for both of us."

"I wasn't really planning to have a large dinner. . . ."

"At times like this, food is a great consolation." A glance at his tall, lean frame made her smile. His was certainly not the physique of a man accustomed to drowning his sorrows in food. As if reading her thoughts, he added, "And it's not as if either of us needs to worry about putting on weight."

"The trials of the job keep us fit," she said lightly.

Taber swept a hand through his dark hair. "I've spent the entire morning dealing with those trials. I've had to redo the whole schedule! I believe I must have called every hotel in Morocco, apologizing in four different languages for the change in reservations." His expression grew serious. "With all the cancellations, this tour is going to be a total loss. Carlson won't be pleased."

"He's not that fierce," Noa said. "But I wanted so much for this tour to go well."

"How long have you worked for Carlson-Rand?"

"It's been my only interest. I worked in the summers while attending college, and full-time since then. My father and Wendell created the tour company together, but Dad was in poor health so he never became a partner."

"I've heard all about your father," Taber said, adding with an ironic smile, "and I suppose you've heard all about mine."

"I know only that he was estranged from the company a short time before his death."

"Carlson didn't tell you all the details? I'm glad." His eyes darkened. "It's not pretty and it's not true."

"What happened between them?"

"Carlson blamed Dad for missing funds."

Taber said the words casually enough, but

46

Noa did not miss the look of pain, a flash of anger in his eyes. Embezzlement was such a serious crime. The reason behind the estrangement was much worse than Noa had imagined.

"I entered this job to clear the Rand name," Taber explained. "Nothing is more important to a Moroccan — or an Englishman, for that matter — than the family honor." After a short pause, he added, "I really admire Carlson for hiring me, believing as he does that my father nearly ruined the business. Somehow I feel it's my responsibility to help him put the tour company back in the same shape it was several years ago."

"What do you mean?"

"Didn't you know Carlson-Rand's been losing money? That's why this Moroccan venture is so important. It has to be a success!"

Wendell Carlson had never said anything to Noa about the tour company's being in financial trouble. She wanted to pursue the subject further with Taber, but they were interrupted. Greg Corbin, looking hurt and a little accusing, stood at Noa's shoulder. "You could have told me you had a dinner date," he said.

"It's not an official date, only a business meeting," Taber replied smoothly, coming to Noa's rescue.

Greg Corbin brightened. "In that case, mind if I join you?"

"No. Of course not," Noa said, carefully hiding her disappointment. "Taber, this is Greg Corbin."

"I recognize the name from our tour list," Taber said. He extended a hand to Greg. "Glad you're joining us, Greg."

As Greg's eyes settled on Taber, they became murky, like restless ocean water. Sensing the tension between the two, Noa was glad when the waiter rushed over. "I'll have whatever they're having," Greg said, without looking at him. "Why two tour guides?" he asked Taber.

"We're starting a new agenda with Morocco," Taber answered. "Noa and I are writing the program together."

"I believe I'll have a little more tea," Noa said, her throat suddenly dry. The waiter had disappeared, but to the left of the table, a few steps away, was a large silver teapot. Noa pushed back her chair.

"Here, let me." Greg started to rise, but Taber got to his feet quickly and, brushing past Greg, lifted the ornate silver teapot from the tray. He held the spout some distance from the cup and poured a stream of tea with a flourish, the way Noa had seen the waiters do at the finer cafés. She marveled

48

that he did not spill a drop.

During the meal Taber and Greg talked more to each other than to her. They spoke of the United States, engineering, and Morocco, in the manner of negotiating enemies trying hard to find common ground. Noa grew more and more silent, resenting the fact that her evening had been spoiled by Greg's intrusion. She was glad when the waiter came with the check.

Taber and Greg reached for the check at the same time, but this time Greg was quicker. "I've got it," he said above Taber's protests. As if to impress Noa, Greg continued, "I'm the gate-crasher here, so I insist on paying the bill."

Greg reached into his suede jacket pocket. Noa saw his face suddenly go pale. He moved his hand from pocket to pocket, looking confused and a little embarrassed.

"What's wrong?" she asked.

"My wallet! I've been robbed!" For a moment Greg looked stunned, then angry. "I had all my cash in it, over six hundred dollars!"

"Where did you go after you left your room?" Noa asked him.

"I came right down here. No — I did stop by the gift shop," he said, correcting himself.

"Was it crowded?"

"Not like it was this afternoon."

"Did you see anyone suspicious in there?"

"Now that you mention it, I saw one of those Arabs — real sneaky looking! You know, the ones who wear those hoods over their heads. He sure looked like a pickpocket, but I know he didn't get close enough to me to steal my wallet. Besides, Cathy was with me. Surely one of us would have noticed."

"Cathy was with you?"

"Yes, she saw me from the gift-shop window and came in. She wanted my opinion on some earrings. After I left the gift shop, Cathy went back up to her room, and I came down here."

The mention of Cathy's name made Noa's heart sink. She thought of Mike's missing coins and the fact that he would never have parted with them. Very possibly the girl had been stealing from Mike, and that was why he had disinherited her. Noa thought of Greg, courteously looking at earrings while Cathy, the person he least suspected, picked his pocket.

The thought filled her with a kind of panic. She should never have brought Cathy along! She should have arranged to leave her in Algeciras with friends.

Noa glanced at Taber, who was taking care of the bill. What was she going to do about Cathy now? Her primary allegiance was to her tour group. Perhaps she should search Cathy's belongings for the money or even confront the girl with her suspicions.

Finally remembering Greg, she turned to him with a flood of questions. "Did you lose your passport? Will the money loss put you in a bind? We could arrange. . . ."

He attempted a grin. "Luckily that was just my spare cash. All my traveler's checks for the trip are still in the room. I'm sure glad I left my passport with them."

Noa's thoughts once again turned to Cathy, so she was startled by Greg's certain, slow-paced words: "It couldn't have been anyone but *him*." Greg's eyes, more green than blue, narrowed as he stared angrily toward Taber. "You saw the way he brushed against my chair when he went after the tea. I think he picked my pocket!"

Noa's eyes widened at the preposterousness of Greg's accusation. "Taber wouldn't —"

"I think I'll call security and have him searched."

"I wouldn't advise you to accuse him without proof. The best thing to do is talk to the authorities."

Taber, striding forward, picked up on her last words. "That's exactly what we're going to do. Noa, I'll take care of this." His dark eyes lingered on her before shifting to Greg. "You just come with me and we'll make a report."

With an angry, sullen look that somehow reminded Noa of Cathy, Greg followed Taber.

Noa remained in the dining room. The richness of the tile, the lushness of the plants, now seemed as unappealing as the tea left in her cup. Mike's death, the problems with Cathy, cancellations that made the whole tour unprofitable, and now this robbery! She could do nothing about Mike, Cathy, and the cancellations. But concerned about the theft and the effect it might have upon the tour, she decided to make a call to her boss.

As usual, hearing Wendell Carlson's deep, confident voice put her fears into perspective. "There are pickpockets everywhere, Noa. Carlson-Rand isn't to blame. It's Corbin's fault for carrying so much cash. He should know better." After a slight hesitation, he added, "You have the same problem your father always had: You assume too much responsibility. The tour hasn't even started yet."

"I have some very bad feelings about this tour."

"Yes, the cancellations are a blow. You probably don't like being left with thirteen. You may have a subconscious superstition."

"I wish that were all it is. What do you know about Taber Rand? I can't imagine why you would hire your worst enemy's son."

"When you live a little longer, Noa, you'll realize that enemies and friends all blur together." He chuckled a little and her heart was lightened by the thought of his bright eyes and amused, slightly cynical smile. "Most of my life I've wondered — whom can I trust?"

"Do you think we can trust Taber?"

"I don't know. I hired him only because Taber and I have something in common: His father got both of us into trouble. I felt a little sorry for Taber."

"He doesn't seem one to inspire pity."

"Life is very complicated, Noa. When I looked at Thomas Rand in his coffin, he seemed to be a dear friend. It was too late to tell him so, so I did the next best thing — I hired his son."

"What do you want me to do about the robbery?"

"Thanks for reporting it to me, but what

can you do? The police won't do anything either, except put the report in a file nobody intends to open. Remember, Noa, we're not to blame. I'm going to be in Morocco soon. I'll contact you along the way." He paused. "How's Cathy? I'll bet she's a lot of comfort to you."

Chapter Three

Of the thirteen people waiting in the tiled room adjoining the hotel lobby, Noa immediately liked the old couple best.

The heavyset lady — she must have been approaching eighty — seemed to radiate joy and enthusiasm. That was certainly not true of the seven young girls between the ages of fourteen and seventeen who sat in a somber row in the back of the room. Marie Landos, the woman Noa had met on the ferry boat, stood behind them, like a warden. Marie's shrewd eyes took in everything in the room, while she continued to impart information to her youthful charges.

It would be good, Noa thought, to have girls of Cathy's own age along. They could not help but serve as a good influence.

Noa's gaze returned to the older couple, Belda and Milton Ward. Belda seemed unconcerned that her gray hair was untidy and her expensive clothes were wrinkled, but still she had about her an air of affluence and abundance. She wore excessive, very large pieces of jewelry. Most noticeable were the huge onyx elephants hanging from a series of thick chains around her neck. White-haired and stocky, her husband — at least ten years younger than she — seemed pleased because Belda was pleased, as if it were his habit to acquire her mood of high adventure.

Because of people like Belda and Milton Ward, Noa loved her job.

Noticing Noa looking at them, Belda said, "I've been on Moroccan tours at least six times. But this is Milton's first trip. This is going to be so exciting, isn't it, Milton?"

"You bet!"

"We're going to the medina, today, aren't we, dear?" she asked Noa.

"We'll end today's tour there," Noa replied.

"Good." Belda cast her husband a playfully defiant glance. "I'm buying all the rugs I want, Milt!"

"I'm sure," Milton said, leaning forward, his heavy stomach straining his tight, white shirt.

Greg entered and seated himself. He seemed less disturbed, as if a night's sleep had allowed him to accept the loss of his money. Casual clothing and the sheen of his tousled hair made him look more attractive than he had last night.

Noa checked her watch. Taber would not be at the meeting. He had told her he would meet them at the bus at nine. It was exactly eight. A tall, thin man of middle age entered, walking with a quiet, almost stealthy step toward a chair in the front. No doubt it was the hooded garment of brown, woven material that caused everyone to watch him. They might have, anyway. He had about him an air of mystery. He made Noa slightly uncomfortable.

"Good morning," she greeted him.

He nodded coldly in response to her greeting. At first she had thought his eyes were brown, but upon closer look they were bluish like those of the Berbers, though his thin darkness was unmistakably Arab.

Everyone was present except Cathy. Cathy knew the meeting time. She would have gotten a wake-up call from the desk. Surely Cathy wasn't going to add lateness to her other misdeeds.

"So we can all get acquainted," Noa said, "I would like each of you to introduce yourself. Tell us a little about yourself, where you live, or why you decided on this particular tour."

The Moroccan stood up first. The woven jellaba hung below his knees, but still revealed dark, European trousers. "Moulay Aziz, from Casablanca," he said with a heavy accent. "I've decided to spend this summer viewing my own country. I hope to broaden my understanding of Morocco so I can best help my people."

The old lady jumped up next. "I'm Belda Ward, and this is Milton. I always have to do his talking for him. He just comes along to eat and pay the bills."

Greg laughed. Milton smiled impishly. No one else seemed much interested.

"We're from London," Belda continued. "We live three blocks from the royal palace. I just love Tangier. It's so outpost British! In my young days, I attended parties thrown by one of Tangier's most famous residents, Barbara Hutton. Would it be possible to drive past her home, Noa?"

"Yes. It's near the Forbes Museum. We'll stop there for a picture if you like."

"I can certainly tell you all about her mansion!" Belda drew in her breath quickly, then gestured toward Milton with a flip of jeweled fingers. "Skip him."

"Greg Corbin, I'm a late-start student studying engineering. I'm from Newark, New Jersey."

"Marie Landos. I'm presently employed by St. Theresa's in Madrid. These are my students Louisa, Carmen, Orva, Agnes, Casilda, Anna, and Eleanora."

Noa gazed at each girl as Marie spoke her name. Every one of them had short, very dark hair, and wore dark clothing. They looked so very alike, Noa wondered how long it would take her to tell them apart.

Noa gave the usual information to the group, gathered tour papers and passports, and announced, "You have about twenty minutes. The bus will be waiting directly out front. We're ready to begin our fun in Morocco!"

Not waiting for the elevator, Noa hurried up the flight of steps to Cathy's room. Cathy sat on the bed retouching her nails.

"You missed the meeting. The get-acquainted meeting is the most important one," she told her niece.

"I'm sure there's no one there *I* want to become acquainted *with*."

Noa had a difficult time ignoring Cathy's impertinence, not to mention the outrageous way she was dressed! The black mini-skirt was bad enough without the tight suggestiveness of the low-cut blouse.

"You should change to walking shoes," Noa advised, glancing at the high-heeled pumps Cathy was wearing. "The streets in the medinas are uneven and dusty."

"I'm not going."

"If you stay here, you must stay in the hotel. I will not have you running around Morocco alone!"

Noa must have sounded as if she meant it, for Cathy rose at once and started resentfully to the door. She reminded Noa of some very spoiled and hateful child as she tossed back her bright, over-sprayed hair and said, "You are going to be so tedious!"

Noa watched Cathy disappear down the steps, then slipped back into Cathy's room. Feeling a little guilty, she first opened the shoulder-strap bag Cathy had left on the bed. She found only thirty-odd dollars inside. Next she thoroughly searched Cathy's luggage and the entire room. She found no trace of Greg's stolen money.

Maybe Noa had suspected her unfairly. She hoped so. Sometimes the girl did surprise her, like the sudden way she had changed her mind about joining the morning tour. Noa had expected more opposition. This quick compliance was no doubt a screen, hiding trouble that was to come.

Downstairs, Marie stood outside the gift

shop in a position that allowed her full sur-
veillance of the seven girls, who wandered
around demurely, not grabbing merchan-
dise, shouting, or giggling. At least Noa
would not have to watch or worry about
them. Marie had assumed absolute control.

She seemed, Noa thought, in control of
everything that went on around her. Noa
stopped beside her.

"Who is that?" Marie asked.

Noa turned to look in the direction Marie
gazed. A man was facing them, his eyes on
Cathy, who was boldly flirting with him. To
Noa's surprise, Marie's critical observation
was directed at the man instead of at Cathy.
"I wouldn't trust him."

He wasn't anyone most people would notice — an extremely ordinary young man,
already balding about the temples, already
slightly paunchy. His only exceptional features were his large, though rather empty,
dark eyes and his very pale skin. He and
Cathy glanced toward them, and he laughed
loudly at something Cathy said.

"It should be a rule that bus drivers don't
socialize with the tour group," Marie said
disapprovingly. "It always causes trouble."

"Bus driver?"

"He's ours. Haven't you met him yet?
Johnny something-or-other. I've heard he

has a wife and kids somewhere in Portugal. He looks like the type who has women all over the place."

Noa saw how Cathy gazed at him, admiring his sturdy chest and thick forearms, oblivious to his flaws. Despite a certain seediness, Johnny did have about him an aura of physical strength that in Cathy's eyes might pass for sex appeal.

"Another thing," Marie said. "You should tell that girl how to dress. Morocco is an entirely different culture. Girls here just don't look or act like that."

Noa was glad that it was nine o'clock. Taber stood by the bus door, helping people up the steps.

"Where's the local guide?" Noa asked.

"Right here," Taber smiled. "Why do you think I'm wearing this?"

He wore a hooded robe, like Moulay's, only his was a rich, woven silver-gray. It made him look taller and grandly distinguished.

"No one knows more about Tangier than I do! Here, let me help you."

"I can manage."

Nevertheless, Taber's strong hand remained on her arm as she stepped into the bus.

Greg was seated in the front, across the

aisle from Noa. She could see his clean, very light brown hair as he gazed from the window to the shoreline. He turned to smile at her, but avoided looking at Taber, who had begun to adjust the microphone.

Taber graciously greeted each person individually, and he kept up a banter with the bus driver, Johnny, as the bus started, moving along a sloping road that made it jog. Noa was thinking with dread of the medina waiting at the end of today's tour. It was so foolish to be this uneasy, to carry childish fears into adult life.

"Morocco is somewhat smaller than California," Taber was saying. "Seventy percent of the people live in rural areas — ninety-seven percent of them are Moslem. You will find many languages spoken here: French, English, Spanish, Arabian, but Arabian is the official language."

As Noa watched Taber, she was greatly attracted to him, feeling captivated by the intensity of his somber, dark eyes. His gaze kept returning to her until, at each lingering glance, she felt a warmth rise to her face. She looked away from him, watched the modern shops slowly yield to residential buildings.

"When the Romans came here they found people they called barbarians — our present-day word is *Berbers*. They are the original occupants of Morocco. Blue-eyed, fair-skinned people, they spoke no recognizable language. No one really knows who they are or how they got here. They are still the majority of the population. The Arabs, you remember, didn't establish themselves permanently in Morocco until the year 788."

"Mrs. Ward has asked to stop at the Hutton mansion," Noa told him.

"An excellent place for a picture stop. It's just ahead."

The bus pulled to a stop near a huge white house enclosed behind a tall wrought-iron fence. It was built high on the hillside; below it were clustered smaller buildings of the same brilliant white.

"Oh, the fun I've had here!" Belda exclaimed. "She was such a dear! See this ring I wear?" Belda held up her hand. Every eye in the bus locked on the massive jewel, a glowing greenish-blue emerald surrounded by diamonds. "I bought this from Barbara Hutton's personal collection! It's insured for $86,000, but it's worth more like $150,000."

Automatically Noa's gaze settled on Cathy. The girl sat forward in her chair as if the announcement had roused her from deep apathy. She was not aware that Noa was watching her. Her eyes did not leave the enormous emerald.

Little escaped Marie, who frowned sharply at Belda's announcement or at what she judged to be the stupidity of it. Noa couldn't tell whether the expression on Marie's face was envy or concern for Belda.

Greg looked at the ring with the same awe as the girls from St. Theresa's. Moulay, however, reacted in a way that frightened Noa. His eyes, ordinarily narrow and evasive, widened at the sight of such wealth, giving him a look of junglelike fierceness.

"Isn't my ring the most precious thing!" Belda crooned, holding the ring out to Moulay.

"Shh — they'll think you're bragging," Milton said.

"Oh, I *am* proud of this!" Pointing with the jeweled finger to the house, she added, "And I'm proud that I stayed overnight in that very bedroom. See, the top floor, third window."

"Let me get your picture here," Milton said. "It's all right if we get out, isn't it?"

Noa, the last to leave the bus, said to Taber, "After what happened last night, I wish she hadn't flashed that big jewel around."

"No one on this bus had anything to do

with the stolen money," Taber answered. "But I agree she shouldn't have brought along such expensive jewelry."

Noa's heart sank as the battered wall that led to the medina came into view. Flashes of childhood terror came back to her — shadowy memories of twisting paths, foreign voices, endless openings, growing fearfully blacker with descending darkness.

No vehicles could enter the old city. Occasionally a peddler on a donkey would go through the arched gate. Failing to catch the high spirits of the Wards, Noa followed the others from the bus.

"This is the most exciting part of Morocco!" Belda cried.

"It's a long, hot walk from here," Taber told Noa, strong fingers tightening on her arm. "You could let me take the group through while you go back to the hotel. You look a little tired."

"And miss your lectures!" Trying to be realistic, Noa used a sort of self-derision to deal with her feeling of sickness.

"Then you bring up the rear and make sure no one gets lost," Taber said. He pushed forward. Soon he held up his hand to stop the small group and point out an ancient mosque with its towering minaret.

"I want to go in one," Cathy said.

"I'm afraid we can't do that. Women, even Moslems, are never allowed to enter the mosques."

"What's fair about that?" Cathy demanded loudly. "I don't like this place already!" She turned to address the seven girls. "We should just demand to go in!"

"Change takes place very slowly," Taber said, giving Cathy an amused glance, "and we are guests. We must be good guests."

As they proceeded, more and more often Cathy and Belda Ward began dropping far behind — Belda, to admire the rugs; Cathy, to attract the attention of the rows of salesmen.

"You'd better keep up with the group," Marie and Noa kept advising them.

Cathy gave Marie the same cold look she usually reserved for Noa when Marie commented, her voice brittle, "At St. Theresa's we teach our girls courtesy."

"I'm not studying to be a nun," Cathy retorted.

"Neither are we," Orva, one of the quiet girls, told Cathy.

"You might as well be," Cathy shot back.

"I see you intend to make this trip very unpleasant," Marie said, bristling.

"I wish you wouldn't —" Noa began.

"And I wish *you* wouldn't," Cathy interrupted her, adding under her breath, "old fogies."

"At least don't be rude," Noa said.

"You're the one that wanted me along."

The walkway twisted and grew so narrow that the group walked for a while in single file. Noa, way in the back, kept her eyes far ahead, on Taber's broad-shouldered back.

Here she was. She'd thought she would never be able to do it! More freely now, she began to gaze around at the hanging brass items, the woven blankets and rugs. Ahead of her an emaciated old man was seated on the ground, crude jewelry and trinkets spread around him. She met his dark eyes and felt a rush of pity.

He selected a silver "Hand of Fatimah" from the necklaces with their chunky, yellowish stones and held it up to her. Noa smiled, took some coins from her purse, and gave them to him. She judged from the light that came into his eyes that he was being well paid. She held the charm for a moment, then stuffed it into her pocket and rushed to catch up with the others.

"Isn't this pattern just perfect?" Belda said to her. "Feel how thick this rug is!"

Noa obligingly fingered the plush weave of the green rug before telling Belda, "We'd better keep up with the others. We don't want to get lost."

Belda looked back longingly as she followed Noa. "That's the prettiest rug I've seen yet! Most of the Moroccan rugs are red or blue. It's so hard to find a green one. Noa, do you think I should buy it?"

"There will be others along the way."

"But that one is almost perfect."

"Hurry." Noa urged the old lady forward. "They're almost out of sight."

When they turned the sharp corner that led to a wide opening, Noa was relieved to see Taber there talking with their group. "Some of you have indicated that you would like to browse. This store is the largest in the medina, one with reputable dealers. After I tell you a little about the crafts, I'll let you spend twenty minutes on your own."

They entered the store through a long passageway hung with fashionable kaftans, jellabas, and other local clothing. Sunlight streamed through open sections of a makeshift bamboo roof. Surprisingly the entranceway opened into a huge modern room crammed with displays and noisy with working craftsmen. Taber stopped beside a bearded man whose quick fingers incised and gilded decorations on leather.

Noa stood in the doorway, listening to

Taber's talk. Every once in a while, his smile, gleaming white against his dark skin, would be directed very personally to her.

Taber moved on, this time pausing beside an elderly man working with pottery. Noa glanced from him back to Taber. The robe made Taber's shoulders look broader, lengthened and slenderized his body. The hood folded back, a perfect frame for the crisp, black hair and the strong features, now damp from the heat.

She looked away again, scanning the room. Greg was inspecting some of the wallets, with Milton Ward giving him advice. Moulay was listening to Taber's words with fascination; Marie and her girls, with studious quietness. But where was Belda Ward?

Noa searched the entire store for her; then with growing anxiety, she headed to the entrance and looked up and down the paths of the medina. The crowd had thickened — hooded figures; men in turbans carrying silver pots and goods; women in kaftans, many wearing veils. Where could Belda have gone?

Noa thought about the green rug that had so attracted Belda. Could she have gone back for it? Noa hesitated a moment, then decided she would have no trouble locating that store and finding her way back again. She walked quickly, ignoring the calls of peddlers. Noises and smells she had not noticed earlier now enclosed her.

At the store, she sought in vain for the lively, white-haired woman. She approached and inquired of a turbaned salesman, who spoke no English. A younger salesman joined him. "Yes. Yes, she was here." He pointed to the green rug. "She was looking at this rug. I turn around once, and she's gone. It was only a short time ago."

For the next ten minutes Noa wandered up and down looking into stores and into the hollows of isolated passages. As time passed, her mouth grew dry, her legs stiff. She felt a return of the panic she had felt long ago when she had run through similar passageways, searching for her father.

The best thing to do would be to return to the group and get Taber or Greg to help her. She hurried back to the sharp turn she was using to orient herself. But before turning the corner, she paused to look back.

To the right, a path opened to another row of stores. Surprised, she recognized Belda Ward strolling slowly along, absorbed in her shopping. Before Belda reached the intersection, a hooded figure pounced from a secluded doorway and struck her from behind.

The old lady crumpled to the ground. Noa raced toward her. The hooded form was bending over her.

"Stop! Stop at once!" Noa called, increasing her speed.

The figure, his face obscured by the hood, lifted his head at her shout, jumped to his feet, and fled before she could reach him.

Noa knelt over Belda. She half lifted her, noticing the trickle of blood that gleamed evilly in the harsh sunlight.

Chapter Four

Belda's hazel eyes blinked, looked dazed for an instant, then focused calmly on Noa. "I'm all right," she said firmly.

Breathing hard, Belda allowed herself to be assisted. Once standing, she swayed a little, rubbing her forehead and testing the sore spot on the side of her head.

"Did you see who hit you?" Noa asked anxiously.

"All I saw was a hood and a face wrapped in a dark scarf." Belda dabbed at the cut on her head with the Kleenex Noa had supplied for her. "It's my fault. I should have stayed with the tour."

"We must get you to a doctor."

"I'm okay. See for yourself."

The cut was deep, as if she had been hit by something with a jagged edge. Swelling and discoloration had started, but Noa believed the damage was slight. Still, Noa felt a helpless rage. How could anyone do this to

Belda! "We'll go back to the group. Taber will want to contact the police."

"I just won't hear of that!" Belda's hand tightened on Noa's arm. "It won't do a lick of good. It will only worry Milton and ruin my whole trip!" She drew herself up determinedly. "I'm just going to tell everyone I fell."

"That's not a very good idea."

"You'd think so if you had to live with Milton. He's a worrier! Besides, whoever attacked me is long gone now." Belda's emerald ring glistened as she waved it toward the endlessly winding walkways. "No one's going to find him here."

When Noa said nothing, Belda added, "It was probably just some mugger after my purse."

"He might have been after your ring."

Belda stared at the emerald. "Do you really think so?"

"It might be a good idea to put it in a safety deposit box. We'll return to Tangier at the end of our tour. You can pick it up then, and not have to worry about it."

"But it's never been off my finger," Belda protested. "If I have to hide it from the world, then what's the use of owning it?" The stubborn resistance, despite the age difference, made Noa think of Cathy.

"Please reconsider."

"No, I won't give up my ring!" Belda began to walk briskly away, saying over her shoulder, "I just want to forget the whole thing!"

"You're going the wrong way," Noa called to her.

Belda turned back with an impish smile. "I'm going back for my rug!"

Noa didn't catch up with Belda until she stopped at the corner booth, the one where Belda had spotted the rug. Belda gazed at the design of the thick, green weave for a moment, then announced, "I'll take it!"

The turbaned salesman grinned widely. Noa waited impatiently as money was exchanged and plans were made for the rug to be delivered to the hotel. Belda turned to Noa with a wink. "At least this knot on my head wasn't all for nothing!"

"You shouldn't have accepted his first price," Noa said. "They always start about fifty percent higher than what they expect to get."

Belda laughed. "My dear, when you're as wealthy as I, it's getting what you want that's important, not what you pay for it."

They walked quickly and in silence back toward the store where the group waited. Taber, his dark eyes worried, left Milton's side and strode forward to meet them. "Everyone's been looking for you. I just hope no one gets lost!"

"What did you mean by running off like that!" Milton chimed in. He did not appear to notice Belda's wound, which she had made an attempt to conceal under her gray curls.

"Shopping. What else?" Belda replied.

"You were supposed to stay right here in this gift shop."

"Oh, this junk's just for the tourists. I wanted something authentic." Belda stepped forward, shaking a warning finger at Milton. "And I don't want to hear a word out of you. Not one single word!"

"I knew it! Just don't even tell me!" Milton rolled his eyes and shook his white head like a playful old lion. "You bought that darn green rug!"

As soon as the tour returned to the hotel, Noa checked the mileage on the bus. This, her last routine job of the day, marked the end of her duties until the group met in the evening for the extravagant welcome dinner in the hotel's "Arabian Room."

As Noa entered the hotel lobby, she saw Greg through the glass window of the gift shop. Though he pretended to be looking at the brass souvenirs, as soon as he saw Noa, his eyes brightened to match his sudden smile.

His reaction gave her the feeling that he had been waiting for her. She was not surprised when he caught up with her on the way to the elevator. "Noa, won't you have some coffee with me before you go up to your room?"

Noa was looking forward to a shower and maybe a rest in the air-conditioned coolness of the comfortable hotel room before the big dinner. She was about to decline Greg's offer, but something in his earnest manner made her hesitate. "I really need to talk to you," he said. "I have something very important to say."

Noa followed him into the lounge, where he ordered coffee for both of them. But when it came, he did not drink, only stared down at his cup, avoiding her eyes with an uncharacteristic shyness. "Noa, I was wrong about Taber's taking my money," he confessed finally, with some obvious embarrassment.

"I'm glad you didn't accuse him, then. What made you change your mind?"

"Well, he's turned out to be an all-right guy, helping me file a report and all." He stirred sugar into the already-sweet Arabian coffee. "It's just that — well, this isn't easy for me to say, but I guess I was a little jealous when I saw you having dinner with him. And I felt that Taber resented my intrusion. He knew I was bound to offer to pick up the tab. So naturally I thought maybe Taber had taken my wallet to show me up, to make a fool of me in front of you."

"Taber would never do anything like that."

"Oh, Taber set me straight when he explained that the two of you were just business partners. I hope what he said is true, Noa."

Anxious to change the subject, Noa asked, "Do the police have any leads on the stolen money?"

"No, but the more I think about it, the more I believe someone in the gift shop must have picked my pocket. Maybe it *was* that guy in the hooded robe. He could easily have sneaked up on me without my even seeing him."

"You know, Greg, you could be right. This afternoon in the medina, Belda was attacked by a figure in a brown hooded robe. I think he might have been after her ring."

The blue eyes widened. "This could be serious. Did you tell Taber or anyone about this? Maybe you should."

"No. I scared the attacker away before

any damage was done. Belda wasn't hurt and thinks this was the work of a common purse snatcher. Now I'm beginning to wonder. . . ."

"If the same person who took my money tried to get Belda's jewel?" Greg ran a hand through his sunlightened brown hair. "Maybe there's a thief working from this hotel. Maybe he followed the tour down to the medina. I don't trust this place anymore, Noa. I'll be glad when we leave here!"

Noa thought with a chill of apprehension that whoever attacked Belda was sure to be leaving Tangier with them. She wasn't at all sure that Cathy was not involved in some way, but even if she wasn't, Noa had no doubt that the thief was someone who had signed up for this tour, and that meant only one thing: Their trouble was only beginning!

As Noa entered the luxurious dining room where the welcome dinner was to be held, she was greeted by a scene that could have come straight out of the *Arabian Nights*. The dinner was to be served in full-blown Moroccan style, complete with music and entertainment. The waiter, in wine-colored tarboosh and robe, led her to a low table where Greg, Johnny Ramos, and

Cathy lounged comfortably upon cushioned benches around the table.

Cathy sat between the two men, obviously delighted by all the attention. The daring black cocktail dress that she wore was too grown-up for her. Noa did not like the way Johnny, the bus driver, eyes already bright from too much liquor, leaned toward Cathy, his hand roaming familiarly across the bare skin of her back. From the nearby table, she saw Marie raise a skeptical brow and realized she was not the only one watching Johnny with a wary eye.

Greg moved over, making room for Noa on the cozy seat beside him. "This is great, isn't it?"

Noa's gaze drifted to a table in the far corner, and her eyes unexpectedly met with Taber's. Surrounded by such Arabic splendor, dressed in a flowing kaftan threaded with gold, he put Noa in mind of some rich and all-powerful sultan. His eyes were bright and smoldering in the darkness, the lashes so black they looked as if they were smudged with kohl.

Her breath catching in a strange way, Noa smiled and waved to him, expecting to be greeted with that flash of white teeth against olive skin that she knew so well. But instead, his black eyes remained cold and unresponsive as he barely acknowledged her greeting. Noa felt her heart sinking. It wasn't like Taber to retreat into dark corners. Why didn't he come over and join them?

The waiter brought a flaky pastry filled with meat and sweet almonds. The low, primitively pleasant sound of a lute filled the air. But the delicious food and the romantic atmosphere were wasted on Noa. She cast a sidelong glance at Taber, whose dark face and glowering eyes loomed angrily in the candlelit glow of the room. She kept wondering what was wrong. What had she done to make him act so foreign and distant?

"I'm not used to eating with my fingers," Greg commented as he broke off a piece of the steaming pastry.

"Just imagine it's pizza. When in Morocco —"

"Do as the Moroccans do?" Greg finished for her. "I'd still trade my gold watch for a fork and spoon."

Noa heard the sound of purring near her feet. Greg noticed the kitten with an amused smile. "We've got a guest," he commented. "I guess animals aren't barred from the restaurants here like they are back home."

"Evidently not," Noa said. The kitten rubbed against Noa's leg, unashamedly begging for food. "This one looks like a steady customer."

"He's cute!" Cathy cried. "I'll bet he's hungry."

Johnny Ramos put a chunk of meat on a piece of napkin and called boisterously, "Here, my friend!" They all watched as the unexpected intruder gobbled up the meat and then, with a cat's usual lack of loyalty, moved on to the next table.

Neither the Wards nor Marie's group of girls were immune to the kitten's charms. With a full stomach, it made its contented way to the last table, where it curled up comfortably on the empty pillow next to Taber. Noa watched Taber stroke its silky fur. She suddenly imagined herself snuggled up next to Taber on the cushion, his lean fingers stroking her neck and shoulders, and felt a tug of envy toward the kitten.

"Look! Here come the dancers!" From the adjoining table, Belda rose to snap a picture of the pretty, dark-haired girls who entered the room in single file. The girls were dressed in what looked like golden bikinis draped with a thousand sparkling veils. Noa was fascinated by their graceful movements as they performed a modest version of the traditional belly dance.

The flashbulb went off again as one of

the costumed dancers pulled a protesting Milton from his seat. "Go, Milton, go!" Belda cried. Clowning, Milton rolled his ample stomach and hips in imitation of the belly dance. Noa thought he looked as if he were trying to balance a runaway hula hoop. His movements attracted the attention of the kitten, which darted out to scamper among the dancers, chasing their long veils.

One of the costumed girls approached Noa, attempting to pull her, as she had Milton, into the circle. Noa firmly declined, unwilling to become the center of attention.

"I'll go!" Cathy leaped up to join the dancers. The dark-eyed girls, delighted by her enthusiasm, began to teach Cathy a few simple moves. "This isn't much different from disco dancing," Noa heard Cathy exclaim.

"She's good!" Belda cried. Her flash went off again and again as Cathy, with some success, copied the dancer's movements. The black dress and bright platinum hair made her stand out, made every move appear exaggerated to Noa. Noa saw Johnny Ramos watching Cathy, his large eyes aglow with desire. "You can join my harem any day!" she heard him say with bawdy loudness as Cathy returned to their table.

"Why don't you dance for us, Noa?" Greg teased.

"Yes!" Belda urged her enthusiastically, overhearing him. "Come on, dear. I must have a picture of our tour guide!"

Greg tugged at Noa's hand. "Come on, I'll go with you!"

Despite her reluctance, Noa let herself be tugged out to the floor. After all, it was part of her job to see that the group had fun. This was a special moment for them, an evening to go down in their scrapbooks and be remembered for the rest of their lives. She would not let it be spoiled by Taber's bad mood.

One of the dancers draped a shimmering veil over Noa's tawny hair. The kitten pounced about, striking out at the hem of Noa's long skirt as she raised her arms above her head and shook her hips slightly. "This'll make a great picture," Belda called. "Smile for the camera, Noa."

Noa instinctively smiled into the lens.

"That's perfect, Noa. Now, don't you move. Greg, you come up and put your arm around her."

Greg obediently did as he was told.

"Perfect!" Belda said with a laugh. "You two were made for each other!"

As Noa glanced away from the flash's

bright light, her eyes once again locked with Taber's. "What's wrong, Noa?" Greg asked as he tightened his grip on her shoulder. "The lights didn't blind you?" Noa, aware of Greg's arm tight around her, saw Taber's dark gaze move from Greg back to her. Then, without another glance or word, Taber stalked from the room.

"It looks as if we've got the table all to ourselves!" Greg said. With surprise and a sense of bewilderment Noa noticed the two vacant cushions once occupied by Cathy and Johnny Ramos.

At twelve o'clock, Noa obtained the key to Cathy's room from the desk. Finding the room vacant, she stopped to ring Johnny's number, which she found scribbled on a pad near the phone. Growing increasingly worried, she returned to the lobby, deciding to look for them one final time in the cocktail lounge.

Inside the dimly lit bar, Noa spotted Marie alone at a table. Marie apparently had a fondness for alcohol, although she never indulged when in charge of her schoolgirls. For a moment this made Marie Landos seem like a great fake, but as Noa hurried toward her, the impression vanished, and Marie seemed, as always, the most self-controlled and efficient woman Noa had ever met.

Marie's cold, knowing eyes anticipated Noa's yet-unspoken question. "No, I haven't seen Cathy," she said, "or that fool bus driver."

Noa sank down across from her.

"I knew we should have been watching him more closely," Marie said. "In fact, I had a little talk with Johnny concerning one of my own girls."

"Do you know anything about him?"

"I've made a few inquiries. I found out he has a wife and two children in Cascais." She took another sip of her drink. "His real name is Juan Ramos, but he thinks the American *Johnny* makes him more attractive to the ladies."

"I'm not sure what to do about this."

"I'd be right here waiting for them to come back. Then" — Marie pushed back the glass — "I'd fire him." Marie rose and conversed briefly with the bartender in French. "Cathy and Johnny were in here about an hour ago," she told Noa. "The bartender got busy and didn't notice what became of them."

Together Marie and Noa searched the area near the hotel, the shops and restaurants that were still open. As they returned,

Marie suggested, "You should see if the bus is still here. If he took the tour bus, then you'll have him."

"I'll go back to Cathy's room first," Noa said.

For a long time she sat waiting in the darkness. Now she understood Mike's frustrated letters about the trials of single parenthood. She felt responsible for Cathy; at the same time she was so worried about her that she thought she could easily throttle her.

Noa was just about ready to go down and check on the bus when she heard the doorknob rattle, and Cathy entered the room.

"Wha— what are *you* doing here?" Cathy's voice was slurred, and her eyes had difficulty focusing upon Noa.

"Waiting for you. It's time we had a talk."

"I don't have anything to talk to you about. Get out. I want to go to bed."

"I won't have you acting like this! Now I want to know where you've been for the last four hours. Who were you with? Was it Johnny Ramos?"

The yellowish eyes focused, became defiant. "It's none of your business. I won't tell you. I'll never tell you!"

Before she could stop herself, Noa seized Cathy by the shoulders. "Listen, do you think this is fun for me? Do you think I like having to watch you every minute when I have an entire tour group to look out for? Why, if I hadn't promised Mike I'd look after you, I wouldn't even —"

At the sound of Mike's name, Cathy seemed to crumple. She shook herself free from Noa, then covered her face in her hands. Warily, Noa watched her sob as if her heart would break. Were the tears real or just another trick — an attempt to gain her sympathy?

The daring black dress and the brightly dyed hair gave Cathy's pale face a look of fragile vulnerability. For an instant she seemed a mere child, so young and lost. "Mike's the only person on earth who ever loved me." Cathy's voice was flat, hollow, as tragic as the huge, yellow-flecked eyes. "Now I don't have anyone."

Noa felt her heart soften. She had thought Cathy hadn't cared about Mike, but she had been mistaken. Cathy must have locked her grief deep inside, hidden it even from Noa. "You're wrong, Cathy. You have me."

Noa reached out to comfort her. Surprisingly, Cathy didn't pull away. For a moment they shared a rare closeness, a new understanding of each other.

"You'd better get ready for bed," Noa said finally. "Wake-up call will come very soon."

"Yeah, and I think I'm going to have one heck of a hangover!"

Just as Noa entered her room, the phone rang. "The lost is found," Noa told Marie happily, then confided to her about Cathy's change of attitude.

"I wouldn't be too optimistic," Marie advised her drily before hanging up.

Noa took the spare keys to the bus and headed toward the parking lot in back of the hotel. The overhead lights cast a dim, eerie glow throughout the empty bus. She took the log book from beneath the seat and checked the chart against the actual mileage. What she found made her heart race with anger. Marie's suspicions had been right! An extra twenty miles had been added since this afternoon!

Noa had started back to her room, when a deep voice called, "Noa, what are you doing out here?"

Taber strode from the shadows of nearby trees toward her. His woven, earth-toned shirt was rolled at the sleeves and open at the throat. The simplicity of its style accentuated his thick, black hair and tanned skin. She was distracted by the sight of him, the way his dark hair rustled in the soft ocean breeze.

"I came out to check the bus."

White teeth flashed as he smiled; all traces of the anger he had displayed at the welcome dinner had vanished. "I thought that was Johnny's job."

"Johnny seems to think his job includes entertaining my niece," Noa said. She told him about Cathy's disappearance, the odometer reading on the bus.

Taber frowned. "That doesn't sound like Johnny. He can be quite the ladies' man, but I've never known him to be irresponsible about his duties. Why don't you let me handle this?"

"No, I'll see to it myself." She studied Taber's handsome face in the darkness. "What are you doing up so late?"

"I couldn't sleep." He drew nearer, his fingers tightening around hers. "Since we're both out here, why don't we take a little walk out to the beach?"

"I'd better not."

"The cafés by the beach are all closed, but there's a vending machine at the edge of the walk. I'll buy you a Coke."

"In that case, how can I refuse?"

As they walked, she confided in him her worries about Cathy. "Maybe I'm too protective of her," she finished. "I just want her to grow up . . . right."

"I don't think you have much to worry about. I believe she's a good kid at heart. In fact, I sort of admire the way she has of standing up for herself." Taber's genuine fondness for Cathy made Noa determined to try to be more understanding of her.

Despite the lateness of the hour, the streets around them were well lit; many of the gift shops were still open. Tangier was restless, never really quite asleep. At the railroad station, hooded figures stood in clusters, waiting for the train. His lean hand tight around hers, Taber led her across the tracks to the beach just beyond.

The view from the shore was breathtaking. Beneath their feet lay a stretch of golden sand; above them the bleached white walls of the old city sloped down dusk-covered hillsides toward the sea.

They reached the empty seaside cafés with their striped umbrellas and stood for a moment near the white tables, looking out at the sea. Small boats bobbed in the gentle waves.

Taber tried the machine. "Wouldn't you know? It's jammed."

"That's okay. I didn't really want a Coke, anyway."

"Neither did I." Noa glanced at Taber's profile, so sharp and handsome in the moonlight. "It was just an excuse to get you out here. This is the Tangier I wanted you to see." His voice lowered, became soft and husky. "In fact, all I've thought about since the day we met is having you here beside me in this place that I love."

Noa thought of the flowers Taber had sent, how she had placed them on her balcony so that whenever she smelled their fragrance, she would think of him. She remembered the nights she had wished Taber was there on the balcony with her, witness to the beautiful sunsets, the flowered path that led down to the sea, the little things that made Algeciras so special to her. Had he longed for her in that same special way?

Taber's eyes darkened. "I was so afraid you'd never return to Morocco. This evening when I saw you with Greg, I couldn't bear the thought of losing you to him when my dreams were so close." Hurt flashed in the dark eyes. "Why didn't you tell me about the attack on Belda this afternoon? What made you confide in Greg instead of me?"

"Taber, I. . . ."

"It's so important that you trust me." Noa was mesmerized by his voice, his eyes. He reached out to her, drawing her close against him. "Love and trust go together. And that's my dream — for you to love me."

As he kissed her, Noa forgot about Greg, her trouble with Cathy, and everything else but the touch of Taber's lips on hers.

Chapter Five

The relief and joy of seeing Cathy in a new light and the wonder of Taber's kiss vanished with the six-o'clock wake-up call. Happiness was replaced by dread as Noa thought of Johnny Ramos and the fact that she must fulfill her duty to Carlson-Rand Tours and fire him.

Wanting to get it over with, she headed directly to the bus where Marie said he could be found. She could see Johnny moving from seat to seat gathering trash into a plastic bag. He met her at the door, his eyes red-rimmed and filled with remorse.

Noa took a deep breath, but Johnny spoke before she had any chance, his words hesitant because of his uncertain command of English. "Mrs. Landos told me what you think, so I know what it is you're going to say."

"How long have you worked for Carlson-Rand Tours?"

"Thomas Rand hired me when he joined

the company," he replied, as if recalling a memorable moment.

"You know you can't take the bus without authorization. What made you . . . ?"

"I didn't take the bus. I would never do that."

"You're the only one besides Taber and me who has a key."

Pain deepened in his eyes. "When Cathy and I left the dance, we went to the bar. I drank too much and passed out. Cathy got in my pocket and took my keys! I know she did!"

From her own experience with Cathy, Noa immediately believed him. "Nevertheless, the keys are your responsibility."

"I know. I take . . . responsibility," he said, stumbling over the word.

Noa made a sudden decision, one she doubted even as she spoke. "This time I'm going to authorize the extra miles. But if this ever happens again. . . ."

"It won't! Ever!" His pale face lit up in gratitude. "And let me tell you something else: I won't be hanging around your niece anymore!"

The thirteen tour members showed up at the bus even before the scheduled departure time, as if anxious to get on to Rabat. Since absolutely no picture came to mind when she thought of Rabat, Noa wondered why she had such qualms concerning the day and their eventual arrival. Perhaps it was enough that it would bring her one day closer to the medina at Fez where she had been lost as a child.

Taber, handsome in a white T-shirt and jeans, was the last to board. As Taber entered the bus, he bent to lift a glistening trinket from the floor. Noa recognized it at once.

"I bought that in the medina yesterday," she said. "It must have fallen out of my pocket."

Taber seated himself beside her, studying the design on the pendant: the outline of five fingers filled with crude circles. The craftmanship was primitive, but the effect was nonetheless appealing.

"A good choice," Taber said. "You should wear it around your neck. The Hand of Fatimah has the power, you know, to protect you from the evil eye."

"I could use some good luck today," Noa said. She felt Taber lift her hair away. His fingers were warm against her neck as he fastened the clasp to the necklace.

"There. That should hold. The chain is nice and sturdy," he said.

Noa glanced at the charm, a tiny silver

handprint against her white cotton blouse. "It's such a stylized hand," she observed.

"That's to avoid the impiety of a graven image."

"Tell me more about the charm."

"Fatimah was the wife of the Prophet Mohammed. Her hand has the power to arrest the evil eye, which is responsible for all bad occurrences. See this?" He indicated a tiny ceramic bead that dangled from the palm of the religious symbol.

"It looks like an eye."

"Right. This eye sends the evil curse back to the sender."

"I hope no one has put a curse on me," Noa replied.

Taber's gaze deepened into hers. "If so, the Hand of Fatimah will surely protect you. To the Moslems, it is a sacred religious symbol."

The bus pulled away from the hotel and traveled a narrow, straight road that seemed to stretch ahead endlessly. Taber soon pointed out a skull propped on a stick in a garden they passed. "The skull of the donkey is also supposed to avert evil. But that is only a local superstition."

"Do the country folk really believe in its power?"

His eyes, almost black, lit up with amusement. "Do you really believe that the number thirteen is unlucky?"

"That depends."

"Depends on what?" Taber asked.

"Upon how the rest of this tour goes."

Taber smiled again. "By the way, Noa," he said in a teasing manner, "if an animal or other creature should call you by name, on no account answer."

"I had no intention of answering."

"Good. It's almost certain to be a jinn, a spirit that can possess even people. You've heard of what you call genies? But don't think they are all good."

"Thanks for the tip. I wouldn't dream of trusting one."

Usually Noa was anxious to begin talking to the group, but today she wasn't. Perhaps it was because she wanted to remain beside Taber. She rose and adjusted her microphone and began her speech, feeling a little nervous. "This time Rabat will be just a stopover on our way to Fez. We will return there and spend three full days."

No cause for nervousness, Noa thought, glancing around. Cathy was sound asleep, and the seven girls, only because of Marie, remained grudgingly attentive. Belda and Milton Ward carried on their own sometimes very loud conversation, and Greg divided his time between Noa's talk and gazing toward the distant outline of the Rif Mountains.

"Rabat is one of the four imperial cities and the main capital. The name goes back to a fortified, tenth-century monastery, called a *ribat*."

Noa was flattered that a woman with Marie's scope would bother to write down the information she was giving, but Moulay surprised her more by his active participation in her lecture.

"Look over there," he said in his deep, heavily accented voice. He indicated a field where two horses, tied to a circular wheel, threshed wheat. "Just like they worked in ancient times. I hate poverty!" Moulay's voice burned with the hatred he spoke of. "I despise seeing my people living so primitively!"

They arrived in the capital city after dinner. Noa distributed keys for rooms, then she lingered in the hotel lobby.

"I know a precious place here in Rabat!" Belda said as she approached her. "Some old ruins. Very few people get out to see them. I'm going out there right away! Milton won't go with me. He says he's played out. You wouldn't believe he's eleven years younger than I am!"

"Aren't you tired after the long drive?"

"I'm perfectly rested and ready for some footwork! I've already talked Johnny into taking me out there in the hotel car. He's agreed to leave me out there to do some exploring and pick me up an hour later."

"Are you going alone?"

"My dear," Belda said, "I was single until I was fifty-seven! I've been a number of places alone. And I like it that way. My first husband died shortly after we were married. He was in politics. I didn't think I'd ever want to marry anyone again; then a year ago, here comes Milton!"

"Is he in politics too?"

"Goodness, no! He's spent all of his life and a fortune trying to establish himself as a painter, which he never did. You could see why for yourself if you ever laid eyes on his work! I don't kid him. I tell him right out, they're just terrible. I said, 'You should have gone into politics!' But nothing discourages him!" She paused for a quick intake of breath. "But he's a dear. Even though he couldn't plan and carry out an afternoon picnic!"

"Would you mind if I came along with you?"

"Of course not!" Belda checked her watch. "I'm going to change. I told Johnny I'd be ready to go in twenty minutes. Bring your camera!"

A few minutes later, wearing pleated, khaki slacks and a blouse with huge, yellow flowers, Belda was waiting impatiently at the entrance. She hadn't taken time to brush back the short, gray hair and now stuffed flying locks under a cap she had probably borrowed from Milton.

"That nice boy, Greg, has been looking for you. I didn't tell him you were coming with me, or he would steal you right away! He reminds me of my first husband, except he has loads of hair and William had none. Come on. Let's wait outside."

"What do you think of Taber?"

"Handsome, for sure! Too handsome! And those Moroccans have more than one wife, remember that! You had best stick with Greg."

"Taber doesn't have any wives," Noa said with a smile.

"You think he doesn't. But look at Moulay Aziz. He has two wives in Casablanca, living three blocks from each other. Here's our car now!"

An angry, sullen look flickered across Johnny's face as Noa slid into the backseat beside Belda, but he said nothing. They left the city, driving on a narrow, empty road that followed the ocean for a few miles, then wound inland. Soon they left the highway altogether, traveling on a scarcely visible trail, which a mile or two later, at the base of a great bluff, came to an abrupt end. "Come back for us in an hour, Johnny," Belda said and slipped him some money.

Belda bolted out and started at once to climb the steep slope ahead. A faint trail was evident through the grass and rocks. "Come on, Noa!" As Noa followed, she heard the spinning of tires as Johnny pulled away in a careless manner he had never dared to use while driving the tour bus.

The air was uncomfortably hot and very still. The car's quick departure left a profound quiet. Noa had expected ruins thick with tourists, not this total isolation. How could she have allowed Belda to come out here after what had happened at the medina? Noa glanced back as the car sped rapidly onto the distant highway, and she felt afraid.

Belda's lithe step had placed her far ahead. She stopped midway to snap pictures. "Now one of you with all those little shacks clustered down there!" she cried.

Noa looked back. Sunlight glared against the white of the tiny houses built on hillsides that sloped toward the ocean. One of the small homes was set by itself where the land leveled, and she could see activity around it. The inspiring view eased some of her anxiety.

She continued her climb. Along the top of the rise, ruined outlines of a once great wall rose and fell. In places rubble was piled in great stacks topped with huge, gray stones that were parts of long-fallen columns.

"The world is filled with such majesty!" Belda said. "Just to have eyes and ears for one single afternoon! What a blessing!"

Slowly the silence around them became pleasant rather than fearful. Noa felt that she and Belda Ward had found some common ground.

"This is why I love being a tour guide," Noa confided.

"I would have loved it too."

After a while Belda started to climb upward again.

"Watch your step!" Noa cautioned.

Belda soon reached the great stack of rubble and stopped to study a huge rock embedded in dirt. Noa joined her, running a hand across the relief carving in ocher-colored stone. "Definitely Moorish," she said. "The Romans did not use that sort of geometric design."

"Wait a minute. I want to get another picture of it. From below."

Slowly now, they made their way over rubble and down into a great area where the earth was sunken and grass covered.

"I always tell Milton, 'You have to use imagination.' Not that he has any. But I tell him, nothing is ever exciting or good or even bearable, if you don't imagine!" Belda drew in her breath quickly, her hazel eyes shining. "Just think for a moment what this great kasbah would have been like!"

Belda circled the area, then followed the wall to a hollowed place under thick rocks, where the glare of sunlight never penetrated. She seated herself on a low rock; Noa sat on the ground, her back against cool stone.

"Here, I brought us each a candy bar," Belda said companionably. "Let's munch."

Noa leaned back and tried to imagine the great, fortified house that had once stood so proudly on this high bluff.

Her thoughts were immediately interrupted by a noise. It sounded very close, but she couldn't tell what it was. It sounded harsh, like rocks scraping together. "Did you hear that?"

Belda, rising, braced her hand against an overhead rock. The sudden movement caused the huge emerald surrounded by diamonds to flash. "Probably explorers, like us."

Noa listened intently, but the noise had settled into the stillness and did not sound again. For a while she waited and watched with a growing feeling of uneasiness, but at last as time passed, Noa became interested in Belda's finds and together they tried to reconstruct in their minds the splendid structure of so long ago.

At length Noa returned to the shade that the thick rocks offered while Belda took picture after picture. She had to admit that this woman, old enough to be her grandmother, had much more stamina than she. "It's late. We'd better start down," Noa said.

"I want to take another picture."

"We've got to go." Noa checked her watch. "Didn't you tell Johnny to be back for us in an hour? He's probably down there waiting. We're already ten minutes late."

"Johnny'll wait. He's getting paid plenty." Belda arranged rocks on the ground that she believed belonged together and snapped a final picture.

Noa waited for her at the edge of the bluff. Going back down the way they had come up seemed the only possible route. The cliff dropped straight down in most places; at least here there existed a trail, however sharply it descended.

Belda reluctantly drew forward. "Did we actually climb that?"

Ascending the incline, it hadn't looked so

steep, but heading down would be a slow and careful process. Not even a tree grew to block a fall, and here and there great rocks jagged upward in a threatening way. "You mustn't lose your footing," Noa said. "Why don't you edge down facing the cliff until we get past the worst of the slope?"

Slowly and carefully they began working their way downward. The long trek had tired Noa. Watching Belda's slow descent, Noa straightened up, running fingers through her sweat-dampened hair.

From the corner of her eye she glimpsed movement above her. She gazed upward. A form in a dark, hooded robe loomed above the pile of rubble. He seemed to have no height or weight, no identity, but floated in layers of hazy heat. She could feel the power of his eyes — evil eyes — staring out from the folds of cloth that obscured his features.

Noa's heart sank. Without conscious thought, she knew exactly what he was doing — prying a limb against a huge stone pillar half embedded in dirt and rocks.

Noa gave a startled cry. At once she slid downward, colliding with Belda. Noa hurled her from the path, springing after her. Both of them lost their balance. At the same time the column of stone crushed against the path they had just vacated, crushed with such force that it smashed into the ground instead of rolling.

The huge pillar missed Noa by less than a foot. Both of them had been but a few inches from certain death!

Noa reached out for Belda, but the cotton cloth of Belda's shirt slipped from her grasp. Belda rolled downward. Noa scampered to her feet. Reaching Belda, she somehow found the power to lift the heavy woman to her feet. "Hurry! Hurry! We must get to the bottom!"

As they stumbled and slid down the bluff, Noa glanced back. No figure appeared along the ruined wall. If they could just get to the car before their attacker could catch them!

The ground soon leveled off so they could run unhampered. Anxiously Noa scanned the area. There was no sign of a car, not on the trail where the road ended or on the highway so far in the distance.

"He should be here!" she gasped. She checked her watch. "He's already twenty minutes late!"

"What if he's come and gone?" Belda asked.

"He's just got to show up!" Even as she said the words, Noa regretted trusting Johnny Ramos. She wondered if he had left them there on purpose to get back at Noa for threatening his job with the tour company.

Tension and exhaustion lined Belda's face. For the first time since Noa had seen her, she looked her age. Sweat trickled down her broad, pale forehead, where gray curls clung. "He's not here! What will we do?" Belda asked anxiously.

"On the way up, I noticed a house closer than the others, within a mile or two. We'll have to get help there."

Gripping Noa's arm, Belda stopped. No doubt she had been hurt in the harsh fall against the rocks. She swayed a little as if she might collapse. She worked the tight-fitting emerald ring from her finger as she spoke. "Someone wants this jewel — very badly! Noa, you must keep it for me! I'll not wear it a moment longer!"

Noa hastened her forward. Not wanting to take the time or make the effort to refuse, she accepted the ring and with shaking fingers strung it on the chain beside the crudely fashioned Hand of Fatimah. She reclasped it around her neck, tucking it under the folds of her blouse.

"I can trust you," Belda said. "You'll be able to protect it for me."

"We'll turn it over to the police or some

bank official until the tour's over. Then maybe all this madness will stop!"

"You do whatever you think best."

Noa kept glancing back over her shoulder. They had reached a section of flatland, empty fields covered with dry grass. With any luck, they would reach the small house she had spotted from the bluff and find some way back to Rabat.

The walk was much farther than she had expected. Like an illusion, the small, white house seemed to disappear, only to reappear in the distance. When at last they did approach it, its brilliant color did prove to be an illusion. What had seemed pure white was really cracked and dirty. A boy on an ancient donkey rode around the yard. Squawking chickens flew from him in protest.

Sensing the terrible dryness Noa felt in her throat, Belda said, "Better not drink the water."

From the doorway stepped a woman wrapped in a dull, brownish robe. As they drew closer, she covered her face, so they saw only great, dark eyes.

"I can make her understand!" Belda said, surging forward to meet her.

Noa did not comprehend any of the words that passed between them. Belda gestured and drew on the ground. At last the boy was called. He urged the donkey away eagerly and soon returned leading two other donkeys.

Belda said, "He's going to take us into town."

"On those?" Noa regarded the old donkey the youth forced toward her. It looked so shaggy and weak. "I'd just as soon walk. But he could show us the shortest way."

"Riding will be faster and easier."

Leaving Noa with the reins to the disobedient donkey, the boy hastened to bring forward a battered bucket, which Belda stepped upon in order to mount.

The heavy old lady looked so funny astride the small donkey that Noa smiled a little despite her fears. She managed to climb upon her own animal, and the boy called them forward with sharp, foreign commands.

They did not head toward the highway, but cut across a rough, dry field, baked hard by the fierce African sun. Walking would be faster and easier, Noa thought, trying to stay astride the bouncing animal.

The worn blanket did not serve as a saddle. She held onto the shaggy neck and thought of the donkey that had carried her from Fez's medina, Dad walking beside her with kindly, comforting words. Noa had sobbed all the way to the hotel. She wanted to sob now.

Little by little the area grew more populated. Even as they passed through busy streets, no one so much as glanced at them. The boy, determined to do the best possible job, led them directly to their hotel.

Shyly he accepted the money Belda and Noa gratefully gave him. Heading away, he turned back to wave.

"We made it!" Belda said, wiping her forehead.

They stood close together, reluctant to part.

"You know," Belda suggested, "we don't have to tell anyone about what happened out there today."

"We were almost killed! We can't just forget about it!"

Belda remained silent for a while, looking down the roadway filled with traffic. "The police won't do anything. It would be a total waste of time to involve them."

"I'm going to call Wendell Carlson. We'll get his advice."

"Okay. I'm going to keep quiet and let you handle everything. I'll just trust you completely. Why wouldn't I? You've saved my life — not once, but twice!"

★ ★ ★

"No, it wasn't an accident!" Noa said on the phone to Wendell Carlson. "There's a big-time thief on our tour! No doubt someone arranged for this tour in order to steal Belda Ward's jewel. We might be dealing with a professional!"

"Noa, take another look at your list! Most of them are young girls, students."

"What do you know about Moulay Aziz?"

"I'll find out about him. In fact, I'll find out all about everyone on the tour, even though I believe I do know what's going on."

"You'd better let me in on it."

"I haven't anything to go on but suspicions. It's nothing I can talk about over the phone."

"Shall I make a police report?"

He hesitated. "Do you know what a scandal would do to our tour business?"

"I don't much care. I'm more concerned about Belda Ward."

"I didn't mean to sound as if she's not my concern too. I just meant that it wouldn't be wise to stir things up. We had better just try to handle it ourselves."

Noa hesitated. Wendell Carlson had always been a strong figure in her life. She had never gone wrong trusting his judgment. "What should I do with the jewel?"

112

"One thing you don't want to do is trust the hotel. I don't know the man who runs it, but I've heard rumors I don't like."

"I won't be able to get into any banks today, unless I make special contacts."

"I wouldn't do that either. Noa, just keep the jewel with you until you get to Fez. I'll meet you there and take charge of it."

"What about tonight? What if someone tries again? Whoever did this will assume Belda still has the ring. I won't be able to protect her."

"Tell her to make sure someone is with her at all times. And, Noa, you bunk with Cathy. You'll be safe enough. Tomorrow you'll be traveling in a group."

"It's very risky. I could just give the jewel to Taber. He seems more capable of protecting it."

Wendell hesitated. "You mustn't do that, Noa. Just don't let the ring out of your sight!"

"But Taber. . . ."

A longer silence followed, "I've just found out some things about him."

"Is it something I should know?"

"There's only one thing for you to know right now: Don't under any circumstance trust Taber Rand!"

Chapter Six

As soon as Noa hung up the phone, she went in search of Johnny Ramos. She found him drinking in the hotel bar. "Why didn't you return for us this afternoon?" Noa demanded.

"What? Didn't anyone pick you up?" Johnny looked up from his beer, the large eyes widening in slow surprise. "I got a message from the desk telling me not to go. They said someone else was coming to get you."

"Who was the message from?"

He shrugged his broad shoulders. Though his stomach was slightly paunchy, thick muscles strained the outline of the blue shirt. Noa could imagine him tugging at the pillar of stone, forcing it down upon them on the trail. "I don't know. I figured it was from the old lady's husband."

"I'm going to check your story out," Noa said firmly.

With a grand gesture that showed neither

fear nor malice, Johnny swept his hand toward the hotel desk. "Be my guest."

The clerk at the desk confirmed Johnny's story by producing a scribbled note written in Arabic. "Saad must have taken the message. One moment." He called the young Arab over.

"Yes, I remember. Someone called the desk with the message. I wrote it down. It says to tell Johnny not to pick up Mrs. Ward and Miss Parker. A car is already on the way. Yes, it was a man who called." He shook his head, "No, he didn't leave a name."

Without a name, there was no way Noa could pursue the matter further. Noa checked her watch, and found that it was time to dress for dinner.

When Noa opened her door, she saw Taber, dressed carefully in a white linen jacket and blue trousers, coming from the room directly across the hall. She noticed how his dark hair glistened as if he had just stepped out of the shower. "It looks like we're neighbors tonight," he said.

Taber's gaze fell to her throat. Noa's heart began to pound so hard that she could feel the weight of Belda's expensive ring against her chest. "The Hand of Fatimah," Taber teased. "You didn't wear it."

"It just didn't match my mood," Noa replied. She had to struggle to keep her hands from instinctively flying up to check the silver chain so carefully hidden beneath her blouse.

"What? Not in the mood for good luck? You look lovely all the same," Taber complimented. "Are you going down to dinner now?" She was aware of his sharp profile, his lean, sinewy strength as they walked side by side, Taber's arm casually tucked into hers as if the two of them belonged together. The feeling of warmth and security was spoiled only by Wendell Carlson's warning. What had he found out about Taber? Why had he warned her not to trust him?

Moulay Aziz, in a dark, woven jellaba, waited in the hallway for the elevator. He followed Taber and Noa inside, then pressed the button.

Noa felt nervous and uncomfortable as the elevator closed its automatic doors. The stress of concealing the ring made her feel as if everyone was staring. Moulay, too, seemed to be watching her out of the corner of his eye, as if he somehow secretly knew she had Belda's jewel.

The hooded jellaba reminded Noa of the robed man Greg had seen in the hotel gift shop before his wallet was stolen, the furtive figure who had attacked Belda in the medina, and the vague form she had seen at the top of the path before the stone had crashed down. Although she reminded herself that his manner of dress was common for the area, she still remembered the feverish hue of his eyes that day on the bus when he had stared at Belda's jewel. She was glad when the elevator reached the first floor.

Because Belda stood alone in the lobby, Noa told Taber to go on into the dining room and save her a place.

"I talked to Johnny before I went up to my room," she told Belda. "He said that he received a message from the desk that someone else had arranged to pick us up."

"Who could it have been?"

"I don't know," Noa replied. "But I believe our being left out there was directly connected to that falling stone."

"Oh, Noa, surely you're reading more into this than there really is. The desk is always mixing up messages. The more I think about it, the more I'm convinced that what happened out there this afternoon was some freak accident." The look in Belda's eyes told Noa that Belda didn't believe a word of what she was saying. It was only a way of brushing aside the whole matter and getting on with her vacation.

Belda's attitude added weight to Noa's burden. "I told you not to be alone for even a minute."

"I'm safe enough." Belda glanced at her ringless finger. "Now."

"No, you're not! We don't even know that the attacks have been made because of the jewel! Someone may have another motive for wanting to kill you!"

"Kill me?" Belda's words were so loud and startled that several people turned to look at them. "The only one I even know on this tour is Marie!" She paused to draw in her breath. "You're surely not talking about Milton. Why, he's the gentlest, dearest man in the world!"

"I only want you to be careful!" Noa told her.

Milton stepped out of the elevator, striding toward them with a playful smile. "I don't want to hear your nagging tonight. I'm going to eat all I want to!" He rubbed his prominent stomach. "I feel as if I hadn't eaten in weeks!"

For the first time since she had met them, Noa noticed that Belda had no rejoinder.

Most of the group were already seated at the long table that had been reserved for them. Taber had saved her the seat beside him, and Belda and Milton seated themselves across the table by Marie, who laughed in a forced, artificial way at something Belda said to her. Moulay sat at the far end talking to Greg, and Johnny Ramos had taken a table by himself. Since Noa's talk with him he had barely spoken to anyone.

Automatically, Noa searched for Cathy and found her among Marie's group of girls. As usual, Cathy wasn't hard to spot. The other girls were dressed in long skirts and demure blouses; Cathy wore faded blue jeans torn out at the knees, a red tank top, and a denim jacket so battered and ripped that it looked as if some maniac had gouged it with a knife.

To Noa's surprise, Cathy rose and changed places with one of the girls so she could be seated next to Taber.

"And here I thought we were supposed to dress for dinner!" Taber joked.

"Stressed denim is in," Cathy retorted. "It's the latest thing from New York."

"I've seen beggars with fewer holes in their clothes."

To Noa's surprise Cathy did not respond with one of her angry, sullen looks, but instead laughed and looked flattered. "Trust me. It's ultimately cool."

"I expect it would be, especially on a rainy day."

Out of the corner of her eye, Noa saw Johnny sneak a look at Cathy. She wondered if Cathy was actually attracted to Taber, or if she was flirting with him for Johnny's benefit. Taber, however, did not seem to mind the attention.

The waiter brought drinks and salad, then the main course.

"Fish again tonight!" Milton grumbled, crinkling his nose.

"Moroccans love seafood," Belda said. "They must know a hundred different ways to cook it. After we eat, I'm going right down to the gift shop and buy myself some cookbooks."

"Don't let her do it, Noa. I'll guarantee you her cooking is worse than my painting!"

Belda waved a fork at him. "No one's going to believe that."

Her unruly hair tamed into a mass of wiry curls, Belda looked cheerful now, as if she had fully recovered from Noa's warning and the arduous trek home from the ruins. "You'll never believe what happened to our driver this afternoon. Some practical joker gave him a message not to pick Noa and me up, so we had to walk for miles, then ride back to town on two old donkeys! Can't you just see us! My backside is still sore!"

"Cute!" Cathy said, laughing loudly. "I

wonder who did it."

Noa glanced from Cathy to Milton. On the surface he seemed to know no more about the incident than Belda had just revealed. She studied his rugged face and mane of shaggy white hair, and thought about what Belda had told her about him. She gathered that the Ward money was Belda's. An unsuccessful painter, Milton must have been glad to meet an older, very wealthy woman to support him.

How well did Belda really know her husband of only a year? Noa found herself studying the heavy, hairy arms, the husky shoulders. He would not lack the strength necessary to pry loose the column for the purpose of killing his wife. Was it possible that he had planned the robbery attempts in order to set the stage for Belda's murder?

She began to listen to them. Their fondness and the banter that never seemed to lag made her feel a little ashamed of her suspicions.

"You're very quiet tonight," Taber said.

"I'm a little tired."

Noa made the same remark again after dinner, when she declined Taber's suggestion that they stroll downtown. Instead Noa searched for Belda and found her, true to her promise, in the hotel gift shop. But she was not picking out cookbooks. She was helping Moulay Aziz choose between an array of bracelets, rings, and necklaces.

Belda motioned Noa over. "We need help!"

Noa approached the glass counter.

"And we think we have problems!" Belda exclaimed. "Poor Moulay here has to bring home gifts to please two women!"

Moulay's dark face flushed in embarrassment. "Last time," he confessed, "my first wife thought I brought home a finer gift to my second wife. It caused much disharmony in our family. I do not wish to make the same mistake again."

Studying the display of women's gifts with such intense bewilderment, Moulay seemed for the first time to Noa to become human. Beneath the cool exterior, the sharp beard, and the hooded jellaba, Noa saw a worried husband, not so much different from the American men who lingered about the perfume counters around Christmastime. Except that Moulay had not one, but two wives to please — and jealous wives, from the sound of it. Noa smiled to herself. Double jeopardy!

"I like this necklace," she volunteered.

"That's a good choice," Belda affirmed. "What woman doesn't like pearls?" Aside to Noa, she commented, "Having more than one wife could get expensive!"

"I'll buy two of these," Moulay started to tell the clerk.

Belda placed a restraining hand on his arm. "No! No! Never give two women the same gift!"

"I do not understand. If the gifts are the same, there will be no question that they are of equal value."

Belda laughed and selected another necklace in lieu of the second strand of pearls. "For a man with two wives, you have a lot to learn about women!"

"I like him," Belda said, allowing Noa to guide her out to the hotel's garden area. "He is so very intelligent! And religious too! Why, he told me when he gets wealthy enough he is going to work full-time to better conditions for Moroccans!"

They found a stone bench and sat down beneath heavy-leafed plants. "What did you do with my ring?" Belda whispered.

Noa brought a hand to her throat. "I've still got it on."

Belda looked surprised and amused.

"I'm going to make sure it doesn't leave my sight. Tomorrow, when we arrive in Fez, I'll turn the jewel over to Wendell Carlson. He'll see that it is transported to a reputable bank in Tangier."

"You're a jewel yourself, to go to all this trouble. It has to be someone in our tour group, doesn't it?"

"I'm afraid so." Noa chose her next words carefully. "Belda, you mentioned that you had a large insurance policy on the ring."

"You surely don't think I . . . or Milton?"

Of course Belda had nothing to do with insurance fraud, not when she had been just an inch or two from death!

Belda patted her hand. "Don't worry about Milton. Miltie wouldn't squash a bug!"

Lugging newspapers, Milton entered the garden, calling out to them. "Belda, let's go on up. I want to read."

Noa, feeling lonely and isolated, watched them leave, and soon decided to go to her own room. Before the elevator doors closed, Moulay Aziz hurried forward. She remembered how he had been waiting outside in the hallway when she and Taber had come down earlier this evening, as if it had been his intent to follow them. Was he following her now? The thought of being alone with him in the elevator frightened her.

Noa glanced at him, and Moulay nodded in a silent, polite way. For the first time, she noticed that one of his eyes was slightly out of focus. He seemed to be looking at her and also at some point beside her. His eyes, with their bluish Berber cast, contrasted unnaturally with his very dark skin, and made him appear sinister.

The elevator reached her floor. Moulay got out, too, but disappeared quickly around the right-hand corridor. Noa stood uneasily in front of her door before inserting her key.

Noa felt her own sharp intake of breath. Someone had been in her room. Nothing had been left untouched, unsearched. A drawer had been opened ever so slightly, and pictures hung in not quite the same position as before. She drew further into the room. Her suitcase, closed and latched, was no longer in the exact place she had left it. She opened it, knowing that each garment had been rearranged, each bottle opened. The sneaky pilfering struck her as more formidable than if the entire room had been vandalized.

"Is there something wrong?"

Noa turned to see Taber standing at the open doorway.

"Someone has been in my room."

Taber crossed to the phone. "I'm going to call the main desk and get security up here right away."

"No, Taber. Nothing seems to be missing."

"Why would anyone search your room?"

She turned away, stuffing clothes back in her case and reclosing it.

"It looks to me as if they were after something in particular," Taber said. "Something small. Jewelry."

Noa heard her own nervous laugh. "I don't have valuable jewelry."

"It's beginning to look as if someone on this tour is a professional thief."

"He would probably think I carry a lot of currency for exchange purposes."

"I don't believe in this case he was looking for money." Taber's dark eyes locked on hers in challenge. "I think you know exactly what he was trying to find."

"What makes you think so?"

"Belda wasn't wearing her ring at dinner."

Noa turned away from the intensity of his gaze.

"Did Belda give you the jewel for safekeeping?"

Noa forced herself to face him. Surely she could trust the concern she saw on his taut features. She longed to rush into his arms and be protected by him.

"Noa, you do have the ring, don't you?"

Only Wendell Carlson's firm warning kept Noa from telling him the truth.

Much too afraid to remain in the room throughout the long night, Noa called the desk downstairs about the chances of getting another room, but everything was booked full. Deciding to take more of Wendell Carlson's advice, Noa collected her luggage and headed down the hallway to Cathy's room.

"Who's there?" Cathy opened the door a crack. She still had on the faded jacket and jeans she had worn to dinner. But upon her ears flashed a new pair of dangly, golden earrings.

"Something's wrong with my air conditioner," Noa said. "I'm going to stay with you tonight."

"Oh, great!" Cathy exclaimed sarcastically, but stepped back, allowing her to enter. Cathy stood pouting with her arms crossed as Noa arranged her tote bag and suitcase.

"I know what you're really up to," Cathy said finally, golden earrings jangling. "You're afraid I'll sneak out again. You're spying on me!"

"Where did you get those earrings?" Noa demanded.

"The gift shop."

"They look expensive."

Cathy shrugged. "They weren't. Not really." Cathy went into the bathroom and closed the door.

Noa frowned, wondering whom Cathy had talked into paying for the new earrings. Johnny Ramos? Or had she stolen them?

In the darkness Noa slipped into the twin bed by the window, her fingers closing over Belda's ring. She thought of the irony involved in her seeking safety with Cathy — the person most likely to be behind these robberies. But surely Cathy wasn't involved in this near murder! Such a young girl couldn't be capable of that — or could she? Whatever the case, Noa would be safer in Cathy's room than anywhere else. The last thing Cathy would want now was an open confrontation.

Cathy came out of the bathroom. "Noa? Are you still awake?"

"Yes. What is it?"

"I don't want Johnny to get into any trouble," she said.

Did the girl really care about Johnny? The thought revolted Noa, but she had to acknowledge the fact that it might be possible.

"So Johnny lied to me. Johnny did take you out in the bus."

"None of this is Johnny's fault."

If only she could believe what Cathy told

her! But Noa had an uneasy feeling that Cathy might be purposefully trying to blame Johnny in order to protect that night's real driver of the bus. Noa thought of Taber, who had his own keys and from the shadows had watched her read the odometer.

An image of Cathy and Taber sitting together at dinner settled suspiciously into Noa's mind. Surely it was of no significance that he seemed to have paid Cathy special attention. Taber laughed and joked with everyone, from gray-haired Belda to the brittle Marie. He only liked Cathy; he was trying to help her fit in, that was all.

Noa recalled Greg's missing wallet, and how tonight Taber had so suddenly appeared at the doorway of her ransacked room, almost as if he knew what she would find. Wendell Carlson's warning flashed to mind. Was Taber not only an unscrupulous womanizer, but also a professional thief? Noa tossed and turned on her pillow, her hand remaining locked tightly around Belda's ring.

Hour after sleepless hour dragged by, with Noa longing for tomorrow and the time when she could relinquish to Wendell Carlson the dreadful responsibility of the emerald.

As soon as the tour bus arrived in Fez, Noa asked the clerk at the main desk to page her the minute Wendell Carlson arrived, but it was almost two o'clock before she got the call.

She found Marie and Wendell in the lounge. Taber stood very straight beside their table, as if he were angry.

As Noa approached, Wendell, with his gallant, old-world manners, rose, extended his hand to her, and said warmly, "Noa! How good it is to see you! Sorry I was detained." His large eyes, often widening with a sarcasm he seldom voiced, shifted to Taber. "Rand has been trying to explain to me why he didn't fire Johnny Ramos."

"He's been employed by us for a long time," Taber answered, assuming all responsibility. "It seemed the best thing to do."

"The best thing to do? Break Carlson-Rand policy?" Wendell's eyes grew larger. They made his question sound mocking and humorous, yet Noa detected a glint in them she had never before noticed.

Marie had evidently lost no time in telling Wendell everything she knew about the Johnny Ramos incident. She met Noa's gaze, unabashed, and finished her drink.

"It was my decision," Noa said quickly.

Wendell looked from one to the other again, a smile touching thin lips. "Are we playing 'Who Takes the Blame? Who has to face the ruthless Wendell Carlson with the facts?' "

"The decision was right," Taber said. He checked his watch, addressing Noa before he walked away. "Our tour starts in ten minutes."

"We'll see you later, Marie," Wendell said. The thin, immaculate owner of the tour company guided Noa through the lobby, and they stopped just outside the doorway, where they could talk in private. The streets were crammed with traffic whose noise made Wendell's voice barely audible. "Besides information about Taber, I've found out some interesting things about our Mr. Aziz. We don't have time to talk now, but what do you say we meet right after your tour, about four-thirty?"

"Fine." With stiff, clumsy fingers, Noa removed the ring from the chain around her neck and pressed it into Wendell's hand. He placed it immediately into the zippered compartment of his wallet.

How glad she was to hand the jewel over to him! How good it was to see him! "So much has happened!" she exclaimed.

"I know what you've been through, dear."

Noa couldn't stop herself from talking rapidly, telling him snatches about all that had happened to her — about the funeral and Cathy, about robberies, about the column and her brush with death. Wendell looked somewhat startled, as if so much information overwhelmed him. Noa ended by breathlessly asking, "What will you do with the ring?"

"I'm taking it right to the bank with instructions to have it transferred back to Tangier. Mrs. Ward can pick it up there at the end of the tour. And I had better get started."

"Can't you call the bank from the hotel?"

Wendell shook his head. "I'll take it down myself. It'll be perfectly safe with me."

Chapter Seven

After turning over Belda's priceless ring to Wendell, Noa expected to feel a sense of relief and freedom. Instead, she experienced an increasing uneasiness. Unconsciously she brought a hand to the chain where the Hand of Fatimah still hung tucked under her cool, cotton blouse. She felt lost without the heavy jewel secure against her chest.

As the group headed through the main gateway to the medina, Noa recognized every detail of the three ornate arches, which resembled giant keyholes. She passed through the huge center archway with dread, assailed by the memory of harsh voices crying out to her, of dirty, grasping hands.

Those hawkers long ago had probably intended no harm, had perhaps even been trying to help a terrified child. But to that child, the voices and hands had represented horror and death; flight had been her only hope.

Just inside the walls, Noa held up her hand for the group to stop. Her voice sounded far away, strangely frightened. "Inside this medina are three hundred twenty mosques, thirty-seven synagogues, and four churches. We will also pass by a ninth-century university, the oldest in Morocco."

Marie looked tall and slender in a long, dark skirt and jacket; she even seemed a little gaunt compared to the plump Moroccan women. She maintained a constant, guarded watch, her hard eyes alert and suspicious. At the same time she conveyed a certain sympathy possessed by the well traveled and well informed. Marie was unawed by the vast medina, by the mass of foreigners. Noa wished for a second that she herself could be so self-possessed, so able and fearless.

Noa's gaze left Marie and went to Cathy. The defiance was more pronounced today; the slightly thick lips pouted. Cathy's heavy-lidded eyes smoldered with some resentment, and Noa knew her niece well enough by now to be forewarned. Surely today Cathy would behave. All Noa needed in addition to returning to the one place she feared most was for Cathy to give her additional problems.

She and Taber took turns speaking. They

worked together with a perfect harmony that needed no planning.

"It's very crowded today," Noa said. "Let's please stay close together."

Taber lagged behind to alleviate her worry that someone would be lost. They moved deeper into the medina, which was alive with noise. People passed them, throngs of people wearing skullcaps, veils, turbans. Noa noticed a huge, ebony man with massive shoulders, and she observed raggedy children. Peddlers called to the tour members; hawkers intermingled with them with wares dangling from bags and gripped in dark hands.

Slim and wiry, Moulay walked beside her. His graceful step seemed always resolute. She cast a glance at him, noting the slightly hooked nose; the sparse, graying beard; and, below dark, bushy eyebrows, the grave, beady eyes that made him seem aloof and unemotional.

"Do you know your way around this medina?" Noa asked him.

"I speak the four languages of our country," he said, "so I can find my way around." He paused, seeming to sense her uneasiness. "You don't like Fez very much, do you? What is it you dislike here?"

"Nothing. Nothing at all."

His sideways glance questioned her answer.

"What is your job here in Morocco?" Noa asked.

"I am . . . in exports," he said.

His pronounced hesitation made her return his questioning glance. The evasiveness of his answer hinted at something furtive, illegal. She wondered what it was he exported. A myriad of sinister possibilities — drugs, contraband weapons, stolen goods — entered her mind. Noa knew that she was probably being ridiculous. Yet Moulay was clothed in mystery, and often his looks or his voice would send chills up and down her spine.

The bold hawkers who followed them had spotted Belda as the most likely buyer. She had a small entourage, each displaying silver teapots, woven goods, and leather for her to examine. Belda was laughing and excited. She was not good at bargaining, but to be a sport, she was trying.

A heavyset man wearing a red tarboosh had become attracted to a broken key chain that dangled from her purse. He fingered the half of a deep red ceramic chicken's head Belda had no doubt purchased in Portugal.

"You don't want that," Belda advised. "It

isn't any good. It's broken."

"I want it! I want it!"

Belda laughed loudly. She, at least, was having a good time. "Well, here you are, then. Have it!"

He snatched the key chain from her and scampered off, gazing pridefully at his new possession.

By the time they reached the first wide intersection, Milton, looking burdened but tolerant, was loaded with purchases.

The cobblestones were hard to walk upon. Occasionally they had to stop and press themselves against walls or squeeze into doorways to allow a donkey, usually laden with slimy skins for the tannery, to pass on the narrow path. The trail rose and descended, following contours of the hillside. In places wide, shallow steps led downward. At night different sections of the town would be closed off by heavy wooden gates. Noa recalled leaning against one of the gates as a child, trying to catch her breath and thinking that if it were only open, she would be safe.

As they continued to walk, Noa, growing more and more nervous, hastened her steps. The high doorways and walls, designed to block out summer sunlight and winter's chill, choked out all but a bare glimpse of the sky. Noa's skin beneath the cool cotton shirt felt damp.

"This must be called a run through the medina," Greg said, catching up with her.

Noa met his boyish grin and tried to slow her pace. Ahead of them a minaret towered, thin and high above the squat, often make-shift shops that interlocked along dark, end-less passageways.

They soon reached a square where the sun beat down mercilessly. Because of the intense heat, Noa sought out the shade in front of a prosperous shop where the name Ali was inscribed on a great brass plate. Once again Noa raised her hand for the group to stop.

Their persistent followers, offering copper plates and teapots, waited with them. With Greg close by her, Noa stood facing a great, battered wall that housed a fountain under a heavy canopy of carved cedarwood topped with curved, green tile. Water from a crude pipe splashed upon blue and green faience tile. The columns set back against the wall were in very bad repair. In places great sections were loose; a large stone that made up the base of one of the columns resting on the fountain had been set back in place in a haphazard way.

"We are in the heart of Morocco's largest

medina," she told them. "One can walk for four hours straight and see only a fraction of the old town. Its maze of lanes and alleys remains virtually unchanged since the Middle Ages."

"Haven't we gone far enough?" Cathy challenged. "This could get boring."

Noa ignored her. "*The Arabian Nights* was filmed here in the old medina."

"Incredible!" Greg, at least, was impressed.

"There are sixty-five thousand artisans working here in this little city behind the walls."

They moved on again. The constant confusion became bewildering, as if all sixty-five thousand were following them, eager to sell their wares. The hassle of calling vendors, the rude thrusting of goods into their faces — Noa's already frayed nerves felt strained.

They stopped in another wide intersection. This time Taber stepped forward to address the group. She listened to him talk about the Moslem religion. Noa peered into the entrance of the mosque before them, past archways to the vast, rectangular courtyard supported by very thin colonnades. It was almost empty except for a man walking barefoot across the center expanse and three men kneeling in a humble fashion upon the thick, Moorish rug, their lips moving in recitation.

Cathy walked up to the doorway boldly. A man in a shabby striped jellaba stood beside the entrance removing his shoes and placing them beside the others there. She eyed his movements before she turned to interrupt Taber's speech. "I want to go in!"

Moulay stiffened at her words. Marie's mouth tightened at the corners.

"Only Moslems are allowed to enter the mosque," Taber said, then corrected himself, "only Moslem *men*."

"Only men!" Cathy bristled. "Just what kind of sense does that make? Do they think —"

"Cathy, just be quiet. Taber is trying to talk."

"I've got as much right to talk as he has! What he's saying is pure nonsense!" Cathy's eyes, glazed in rebellion, sought out the seven girls who shrank behind Marie. "Let's show them, guys!" she dared them. "Let's show them we're as good as they are!"

"That's not the reason," Taber started to explain.

The girls made no move to join her.

"She's only trying to cause trouble," Marie informed them.

"If you listen to her, you're never going to get equal rights, or anything else!" Cathy yelled.

"Cathy!" Noa remonstrated.

"It's just an old building. Why can't I see it?" She whirled back to the entrance and, with a toss of bright hair, marched through the archway.

"You can't go in there!" Noa called after her. "You'll cause us all sorts of trouble!"

"Try and stop me!" she retorted.

Taber reached Cathy before Noa did. He yanked her back through the doorway. Cathy shrieked and kicked out at him. The blow from her narrow-toed shoe landed just above his ankle, but he didn't cry out in surprise or pain. In fact, he laughed as if the scene amused him. Hastily he stepped forward and swept Cathy off the ground into his arms.

"Let go of me! You have no right!" she shouted.

"We're going back to the bus," he said as he walked by Noa.

The surprised group gazed after them in disbelief. At first Cathy's free hand pounded Taber's back, then she ceased struggling. Was that what Cathy had wanted all along — to be singled out, noticed, by Taber Rand?

Noa felt a pang of jealousy. Taber was

holding Cathy so close! Was he thinking of her as a child or as a woman?

Why was she feeling anger at Taber? She should be grateful that he had managed to save them all from some bitter and ugly confrontation.

The hotel clerk, spotting Noa, came quickly around the desk. "Miss Parker, Dr. Hajji has been trying to reach you. It's about Wendell Carlson."

His grave, formal words jolted her like a physical blow. Noa felt her legs weaken and she grasped the nearby column for support.

"Dr. Hajji's message was for you to contact him at once." She listened to the clerk's directions to the hospital, all the while condemning herself for having allowed Wendell to take the jewel and place himself in such danger! Noa had seen for herself the brutality of the jewel thief. Whoever intended to steal the ring wanted it badly enough to maim, to kill! Whatever had happened to Wendell was her fault for not convincing him of the risk!

Sitting in a cab, Noa leaned forward, both hands gripping the back of the front seat, as if her watching their swerving maneuvers through the crowded street was necessary to ensure their quick arrival.

142

She raced up the hospital steps and, out of breath, faced a young man in white. "Wendell Carlson," she gasped. Her words trembled and ran together. "What has happened to him? Is he going to be all right?"

The man she addressed did not understand her questions. He waved a hand to silence her, lifted the phone, and made a call that brought another, older man into the room. He spoke in choppy English. "Carlson. Down the hall. End." He gestured to the right. "This side."

"What is his condition?"

"Dr. Hajji will soon speak with you."

Noa noticed first the purple bruise on Wendell's temple below the white bandages that crisscrossed his head. Pale and thin, he lay very still.

This man was so important to her life! She couldn't even remember the time he hadn't been there assisting her, so generous in his opinion of her abilities and accomplishments. What would owning a share of the tour company be without his blessing? A goal she did not even want! He couldn't just slip away, the way Mike had, when she least expected it!

Noa blinked and tried to combat the tears brimming in her eyes. Despite her willing them not to, they rolled in hot trails down her face. She wiped them away impatiently, leaned over, and called his name. There was no response.

After a while she sank into the uncomfortable chair beside his bed. The room grew stiflingly warm as the stillness intensified, magnifying the sound of her friend's slightly labored breathing.

What chance had Noa of finding out who had attacked him? Wendell's fate was out of her hands, like Belda's precious jewel!

Noa's eyes from time to time returned to Wendell, anxious for some movement, some change. Occasionally she thought she detected some slight sign of consciousness. Several times, she rose and called to him. Other than a slight tightening of the deep lines at the corner of his eyes and around his mouth, he didn't respond.

A strange feeling possessed her: He was only pretending. She tried to set aside her conclusion, label it as impossible, as stupid, as the result of her over-anxiety. But it remained with her until she actually wondered why he was putting on this act.

She must stop imagining things. If he had wanted to avoid speaking with her, he would not have sent for her in the first place.

She sat down again, lifting a paper from the stand, but not looking at the pages. She couldn't read Arabic, anyway.

The feeling persisted that Wendell was alert, that he knew she was in the room. She called his name again just as the doctor entered. He looked very old, stooped, and slow. He addressed the nurse who accompanied him in Arabic, but in perfect English said to Noa, "I am Dr. Hajji."

"I'm Noa Parker."

"He kept asking for you. Are you his daughter?"

"No, he has no close relatives. Do you know what happened to him?"

"As you can see, he was very badly beaten. Other than that, he told us nothing."

"What is his condition?"

"To begin with, he is not in good health."

"Will he be all right?"

She wanted so much to be reassured, but he said nothing to quiet her fears. "These things are often difficult to predict. I thought at first we were going to lose him, but he has stabilized."

"Who found him?"

"A shopkeeper named Ali Balsam."

"Doesn't he deal in brass? I think I saw his store today. About a quarter of a mile inside the medina, isn't it? By the fountain."

"Across the way."

What had Wendell been doing in the medina? For a moment suspicion overwhelmed her. What was she thinking about her dearest friend and Belda's lost jewel?

"Ali Balsam talked with the police. He said he witnessed nothing of significance."

Silently Noa watched the doctor finish carefully checking Wendell. "I'm going to remain here with him," she said as he started to leave. She was grateful that the doctor offered no protest. When she was able to talk to Wendell, everything would clear up. He would tell her why he had not gone directly to the bank with the ring.

After a while she became aware of someone standing in the doorway. Nerves on edge, she jumped to her feet. Marie's determined step brought her to Wendell's bedside. Her critical survey ended with her declaring, "He's going to be fine. He might not be so strong physically, but mentally he's a giant!"

When Marie turned, she seemed slightly less worldly, a great deal less in charge. Noa even thought she saw a momentary reflection of her own fear in the ice-blue eyes.

"You know that Wendell and I go back a long way," Marie said. "I went to college with his wife. Ann was my best friend." She glanced from Wendell's face back to Noa. "He loved her so much. Of course I did too.

We always make it a point to meet in London at least once a year and visit her grave."

Suddenly, as if disgusted with herself for giving in to sentiment, she spoke harshly. "I knew that fool Belda Ward would bring us to this!"

"Did you know the Wards before the tour?"

"Doesn't all Europe? And most of Asia. That silly old lady drips money and jewels all over the place, and takes absolutely no responsibility. And then Wendell pretends he's John Wayne and rides in to save the day!" she added bitterly.

Marie stopped short. She gazed again at Wendell's immobile form, reached out, and gently touched his shoulder.

Noa found what she was seeing almost unbelievable: This tower of strength was on the verge of toppling.

Noa rose. "Shall we get some coffee?"

Their steps sounded loudly in the quiet corridor. Noa believed she had seen through Marie's crust of artificiality — the heart of Marie Landos was anything but fake.

By the time they reached the cafeteria, Marie, fully recovered, ordered small cups of Arabic coffee and little cakes.

Once seated at the small table, Marie said, "I spoke to Wendell before the tour, right after you did today." With a quick motion she snapped open her shoulder-strap bag. "Wendell said he had forgotten to give you a letter. He thought it was an important one. I was going to give it to you on the tour, but it completely slipped my mind. Anyway, here it is."

Noa immediately recognized the large scrawl which read *To Noa.* Mike! She wanted to tear open the envelope, but she wouldn't be able to bear reading her dead brother's letter in front of Marie. Placing the envelope so it was half concealed under the cake plate, Noa sipped the strong coffee with shaking hands.

"I had no idea Wendell and you were such good friends," Noa said. Her words sounded forced and strained.

"Wendell goes to Monaco often. He likes to gamble and always takes me along."

"I wouldn't have taken you to be a gambler."

"Oh, I'm not. Believe me, I don't appreciate the odds. I just watch. We were there in March."

Dreading the threat of silence that loomed over them, Noa asked, "Does he win much?"

148

"Wendell is so brilliant. You wouldn't think he'd be fooled by those racketeers. But Wendell is just another sucker." Marie smiled, fondness mixing with cynicism. "Sometimes I have to drag him from the tables. That's why he takes me along. I can say no for him."

Marie drank her coffee quickly. "Wendell tells me that if I could speak only one word of English, I'd choose the word *no*. I believe that's a fair assessment."

Marie didn't linger after those clipped words. She pushed back the cup and announced, "I'm going back to Wendell's room."

"I'll sit here awhile."

The envelope wasn't sealed, but as soon as Marie was out of sight, Noa ripped it open and unfolded the paper.

Dear Noa,

By the time you get this letter, I will be buried, and my last will and testament will be known to you. You will, I know, have Cathy with you in Spain or wherever your travels take you.

There are things I should have told you. How hard it is for me to write them; still, it is easier than speaking them to you!

You have no doubt believed I have left all

my holdings to you because of Cathy's immaturity, because I trust totally in your judgment and fairness. However, it is not right for me to leave it at that.

I can't write of the endless trouble, the endless fights that Cathy and I have had. I have tried and failed — I can't do anything with her. I blame him, the so-called boyfriend who has taken control of her mind. Still the truth is that Cathy is a thief. She has stolen everything from me she could get her hands on, including the coins I have collected and treasured throughout my whole life.

I cannot understand such deceit. Do I forgive her? Yes. Because I love her in spite of everything. She is my little girl.

I am leaving this letter with our dear friend Wendell. He will give it to you after I am gone. My death — another thing I have kept from you — is inevitable.

Have I tricked you? Yes. My greatest wish is for you to take Cathy and influence her, make her someone to be proud of, like you.

You, my sister, are the very greatest friend I have had in my lifetime. I am depending on you now.

Mike

Noa reread the letter, then laid her head on the table and sobbed.

Chapter Eight

"My body may be at death's door," Wendell said as Noa entered his hospital room the next morning, "but my mind is still ambitious."

"This sounds like a Shakespeare play," Noa said with a laugh, relieved to see him sitting up in bed, the familiar, sardonic light glowing in his eyes. "Where doth such ambition lead?"

"To one question," he answered promptly. "Will you become my business partner?"

The dream of Noa's whole life was now ever so casually being offered to her. She thought of all the times she had longed for the financial backing to achieve part ownership of Carlson-Rand Tours. Once she had even considered asking Mike to help her. Now that she had the cash it took to say an immediate yes, she was surprised at her hesitation. "Why have you suddenly decided to take on a partner?"

"Health problems. Other matters I

haven't wanted to worry you with. I'm going to have to lighten my work load. That's why I hired Taber Rand. These past few months, I've needed Taber's assistance more than I care to admit."

"Have you asked Taber to become a partner?"

Skillfully Wendell evaded the question. "I always wanted for your dad and me to run the business together. I even told him I'd secure loans for him, but he wouldn't throw in with me without what he called sufficient and proper backing. My life would have been less painful if he had — without the Thomas Rand experience. But that's in the past. Noa, money is no object with you. I know Mike left you more than the amount we're talking about."

Noa's mind flitted to the letter Mike had left with him, to the unsealed envelope. No, she told herself sternly, Wendell Carlson wasn't a reader of other people's mail.

Wendell studied her with arched brow. "What's wrong, Noa? I thought you'd be glad to accept my offer."

"Right now, we have so much else to discuss."

In the stillness that followed, Wendell's eyes widened. That was part of his persuasive charm. He seldom, if ever, applied pressure. She had witnessed the numerous times he had profited by his silences. She believed his business had flourished as a direct result of the power of his personality, which she had always believed to be entirely sincere. Now she wondered for the first time if his charm was simply a tool used to achieve some scheming end. "I'll need to think about it," she said.

"While you're thinking, I'll just call the home office and supply you with figures. The facts of Carlson-Rand you already know." His voice became mocking. "Just in case you don't intend to spend the rest of your life loafing around the Riviera."

"Do you think I have the experience necessary for the job?"

Silence again, followed by the same widening of his eyes. "Ann always grieved because she couldn't give me a son. I did, too, until I first saw you," he said slowly and emphatically. "You are my chosen, the one to whom I intend to pass my torch — if you'll allow Shakespeare a cliché."

"It's your script." Noa laughed again, convinced of his sincerity and feeling more than a little honored that such a man as Wendell would consider her a daughter, one preferable to any son he could imagine. "But for the time being I'm more interested

153

in what's going on on this tour. Tell me everything that happened before you were attacked."

"I should have gone directly to the bank, but I had to see Ali Balsam about a business deal we're cooking up, so I stopped by the medina on the way."

She realized now how little she had impressed upon him the great danger involved in transporting Belda's ring. He probably had attributed her rambling talk of lurking thieves and falling columns to a wild imagination. How lucky she was that he had not been killed!

"Can you tell me anything at all about your attacker?"

"Nothing much. He wore a dark, hooded robe, and I believe he also had a black scarf wrapped around his face, though I wouldn't swear to that. I had walked past the fountain. He rushed at me from behind and I remember two blows."

"What did he hit you with?"

His eyes narrowed in concentration. "I'm not sure, but I believe it was a chunk of rock. Maybe a cobblestone from the path."

"Were there any witnesses?"

"At that moment, the clearing was deserted. Ali found me. He said a crowd had gathered around me by that time."

"Did they take only the ring?"

"My billfold, too, where I had put the emerald for safekeeping. The wallet itself had only fifty or sixty dollars in it. They found it tossed nearby."

"What do you make of it?" Noa asked him.

"Robberies occur more frequently here than they used to. The police believe it is just another one of them." Wendell's alert eyes strayed to hers. "Of course it's someone on the tour who knew you gave me the ring."

"Yesterday you were going to tell me something about Taber."

"You remember Clyde Graham, retired from Scotland Yard? I hired him over a year ago to investigate the company's missing money." Wendell smiled. "Graham's an Englishman. He's never been able to let go of it. When I hired Taber he was furious. He said he was working with the idea that Taber received the vast sums his father had embezzled." Wendell paused. "That would make Taber an accomplice."

"Surely not."

"I hired Taber in haste," Wendell said with that sudden widening of his eyes. "The way things are going, I might not have the leisure to repent of it."

"Do you really believe —"

"I don't know what to believe. Graham called early this morning. He's flying in tomorrow with what he calls a breakthrough."

"Did he tell you what?"

"He wouldn't talk about it on the phone. He did tell me some other things."

"What?"

"I've had him run a check on the whole tour list. This Greg Corbin who claims to be a student at Newark College of Engineering has in fact never enrolled. They've never heard of him. And Moulay Aziz was picked up at Heathrow in January for trying to leave the country with a great sum of undeclared cash."

"Do you think he's a smuggler?"

"Graham thinks he's some sort of political activist. But he could be an international jewel thief instead."

"What about the others?"

"Belda Ward has the record of a saint — feeds the hungry, patronizes the arts. Milton was one of her down-and-outers. He's been married four times, which is insane, but not criminal," Wendell said with a short laugh. "And Marie is in our camp. I've demanded that they search all members of the tour."

"Which wasn't such a good idea," a voice from the doorway admonished. Taber strode into the room. His solemn, harassed manner made Noa wonder how long he had been standing outside the door. "Some of them raised a terrible fuss. Especially Milton Ward. That man has a nasty temper! And Moulay Aziz is threatening to bring suit against us."

Wendell closed his eyes. "My day is complete. You resolve these problems, Rand. That's why I hired you."

"Did the police find anything?" Noa asked.

Taber looked from Wendell to her and answered with a searing gaze and a question of his own. "Did you believe they would?"

"Whoever stole it," Noa said, "would not have the ring. He would be smart enough to hide it."

"You're right. They've gone over the hotel like a swarm of bees over honeycombs. Nothing."

"The thief wouldn't hide the ring in the hotel," Noa said, rising, "but there are other places to look."

Noa decided she must talk to Ali Balsam herself, and that meant going alone into the medina. Street peddlers carrying leather goods and postcards swarmed beneath the huge stone archway. Someone tugged at her arm, proffering a billfold that made her think of the one stolen from Wendell that the thief had cast aside. Impatiently Noa waved him away and began to walk faster. As if recognizing her mood, others who had started to follow her fell back.

The thought of getting lost in the maze of winding alleys and passageways of the medina made her chest tighten with apprehension. She couldn't possibly lose her way, Noa reassured herself. After all, she had been by the brass shop with the tour group only yesterday.

The streets grew tight and narrow. Every turn of sharp, jutting passageway brought some unexpected, often unpleasant surprise — the sight of goats' heads strung in rows in the open-air market, the scent of strong spice, a call of "balak" forcing Noa to press herself tightly against thick walls.

The sweep of long robes and the surrounding echo of footsteps made Noa feel uneasy. Once or twice she looked over her shoulder, certain she was being followed. Long afternoon shadows played upon the old walls, making the shop entrances appear dark and sinister.

Wendell did not often use poor judgment, but his entering this medina with the emerald had certainly been foolish unless. . . . Noa felt herself gripped by anxiety, the same kind that had possessed her in the hospital when she had sincerely believed Wendell was only pretending to be unconscious. Quickly she checked her thoughts. If she couldn't trust Wendell, she could trust no one!

Since she had read Mike's note, Noa had been too sick at heart to think of Cathy at all. Now she admitted to herself what must be the truth: Cathy was a thief — *the* thief. But the girl had to be working with someone else. Noa could not imagine Cathy, who squealed at the sight of a cut finger, capable of carrying out the vicious attacks on Belda and Wendell.

The crowd thinned as Noa reached the place where the cobblestones grew rough and uneven, where primitive steps slanted downward. Tall, sand-colored buildings rose high on either side of her, nearly blocking out the sun. The uneasy sensation that someone was dogging her steps intensified. Nervously she glanced back again, but saw no one.

She had at last reached the clearing where the tour group had rested yesterday. The bare outline of the distant minaret against the sky towered as a familiar landmark. Noa spotted the great stone fountain. Ali Balsam's shop stood only a few steps away.

Her eyes dropped to the packed sand between fountain and store. A clear imprint, a dark stain, remained: Wendell's blood!

Why hadn't the police found a weapon, tossed aside as the billfold had been tossed? Her gaze roamed over walls worn so smooth she could see portions of ancient herringbone brickwork preserved beneath the plaster. She glanced back at the cobblestone walkway behind her; centuries had pounded the rocks so solidly they could have been set in cement. Once again a dreadful doubt washed over her, and she questioned the credibility of Wendell's story. Had gambling and mismanagement placed him in such financial jeopardy that he had staged his own beating to cover up his involvement in stealing Belda's jewel?

No! Cathy, large and strong for a girl, could certainly have wielded the weapon. Or if she was working with someone, he may have used some object found in Ali Balsam's shop, an object he returned.

Thick bars enclosed the windows and huge doorway of the shop. Through them Noa could see polished brass items and curved Moroccan daggers gleaming wickedly in the dimness. A loud jangle of bells sounded as she entered.

Trying to adjust her eyes to the dim

lighting, Noa stepped into a great expanse of tiled floor on which were huge, heavy glass cases containing masses of expensive jewelry and antiques, signs of opulence not expected in the medina. What rare treasures were locked and hidden beneath the counters? Noa would not have been surprised to have discovered Aladdin's magic lamp buried in some dark corner.

"May I help you, miss?"

Noa started. Her thoughts seemed to have caused the thin, turbaned man to appear with the suddenness of a genie from the depths of the shop. Behind him, dangling glass beads swayed, revealing the entrance to a dark anteroom.

"I'm Noa Parker. I work for Wendell Carlson. Are you Ali Balsam?"

A golden tooth glittered at the corner of his mouth as he smiled and said rapidly with a strong accent, "Yes, I am Ali. How is our friend?" The small, pointed beard and glittering tooth made Noa think of a Barbary pirate; the shop might have contained a pirate's plunder.

"He will recover. The police say you were the one who found him."

"Yes." Ali nodded, his black, darting eyes inspiring suspicion. "He was coming by to see me. Wendell and I have, how do you say?" He smiled widely. "We have much business interests together."

"What kind of business?"

"Oh, Wendell and I are brothers. Just like brothers. For twelve years I say to him, bring your tour down here to Morocco — make riches for both of us. Yesterday morning he called me. We will talk, he said, about his bringing me trade from his tour in exchange for a commission. It is good deal. Good for me, good for him." Ali spoke rapidly, as if warding off unspoken accusations. Noa found it difficult to follow his quick, sometimes imprecise words.

Once again Noa glanced around the shop, then back at the sleazy Ali Balsam. He looked much more like one of the forty thieves than like his namesake, Ali Baba. Black-market dealings would definitely suit him, she thought, and wondered why Wendell would consider doing any business with him. Wendell had a soft spot for the unfortunate; most of the stores on his tour stops were run by poor but honest men of the struggling class.

"So you've known Wendell a long time."

Before Ali could answer, sounds of jingling beads caused him to turn. A man's muffled voice called, "Ali, old buddy, where have you hidden the beer?"

"I am a Moslem and I do not drink," Ali said to her, "but I keep beer on hand for my buddy."

The word *buddy* sounded so foreign to Ali's lips that Noa smiled — but her smile faded abruptly when she recognized Johnny Ramos!

At first Johnny glared at her, then he attempted to cover his displeasure with a wide smile. "Ali and I are old pals," he announced loudly, as if trying to explain away his almost incriminating presence. Were he and Cathy . . . ?

Johnny lumbered forward, stopping to drape a hand around Ali's thin shoulder.

"Johnny is, what do you say? Best buddy," Ali proclaimed.

"And he introduced you to Wendell."

"No, that was Thomas Rand. We were business —"

"Associates," Johnny filled in, walking away from them.

"Associates for years and years," Ali said. "He and his son, Taber. Taber buys from me," he added proudly. "Just last month Taber brought his wife in and bought a sapphire necklace for her."

"Wife?" Noa repeated. "Taber isn't married."

"Girlfriend," Johnny again filled in. "He messes up on words."

Of course a handsome man like Taber would have women friends. Still, Noa felt a rush of jealousy.

Johnny spoke again. "Lies do get started," he said. "Like with me. This Marie Landos has been telling things about me that aren't true. She tells everyone I'm married."

"And he's really, what do you say? Engaged."

"Separated," Johnny corrected.

"Nothing is Johnny's fault. Girl didn't know she had a good man, that's all," Ali asserted.

Johnny watched for Noa's reaction through heavy-lidded eyes. He probably thought he was being sexy, but to Noa it made him appear even duller.

When Johnny stepped closer to her, his thumbs hooked into the loopholes of his tight jeans, she instinctively moved away, closer to where Ali now stood polishing a brass plate he had lifted from the table.

Although Johnny's stomach was paunchy, his neck and shoulders were thick and strong. She noticed his forearms, so large, so muscular, easily capable of prying loose heavy columns or beating a man senseless. In this new environment, he seemed foreign to her, threatening. She felt suddenly afraid of him.

"You shouldn't be out here all by your-self," Johnny said.

Seeking protection from Johnny's bold, suggestive gaze, she addressed Ali. "I was hoping you might know of some reason for the attack on Wendell Carlson."

"You know why," Johnny interrupted. "They wanted the Ward ring."

"Did you see anyone or anything that might help us find the attacker?" she asked Ali, ignoring Johnny.

Ali's eyes drifted to Johnny before he spoke. "We are . . . what do you say? Cor-rupted. The medina is not safe, like it used to be." The brass plate resounded as he slammed it down on the table. "I would like to find this man myself!" he said, eyes no longer conspiratorial, but bright with a de-sire for vengeance. "I would take care of him in the old way!"

Ali lifted a statuette from the table. Wasn't it made of stone? Noa's eyes rose again to Ali's cruel gaze and she could well believe him capable of striking down Wendell himself and taking the ring. Maybe Johnny and he worked together — or maybe there were more than two of them. At any rate, she was afraid of them both.

Johnny had moved toward the front door, Ali between her and the back entrance.

Noa suddenly felt trapped.

"If you hear anything, will you let me know?"

"Of course."

Noa drew a deep breath and passed close by Johnny, smelling the alcohol on his breath. He stood leering at her, but made no effort to stop her as she left the store.

"I shall pray for our friend," Ali called after her. "Tell Wendell I will pray to Allah five times a day."

Lowering shafts of sunlight announced the lateness of the hour. The thought of being caught in the medina alone with dusk steadily approaching made Noa hasten; still, she paused for a moment near the tiled fountain.

The thought of Wendell, badly hurt and bleeding, lying near the fountain, made her shiver. Why hadn't he gone straight to the bank with Belda's jewel? Why had he risked his life to talk to some shady brass merchant about a small-time commission deal? Noa wondered who had beaten him so severely. Who, besides she and Marie, had even known that he carried the jewel?

Lost in thought, Noa moved down the dark, winding path of the medina. Surely Wendell would not have told Johnny or Ali Balsam about the ring. Noa remembered

Ali saying that Wendell had called him earlier. An ugly thought suddenly entered Noa's mind. Wendell might never have intended to take the jewel to the bank in the first place! All along, Ali Balsam's shop could have been his destination. Had he planned to turn the ring over to Ali to sell for him on the black market?

Marie's talk about Wendell's gambling and Wendell's unexpected interest at the hospital in having Noa for a partner sprang to mind. The tour company was Wendell's life. If his debts were heavy enough to jeopardize Carlson-Rand Tours, Noa knew he might go to any length to save it.

No! Nothing could ever convince her that Wendell would do such a thing.

Noa thought again about Johnny and his connection with Cathy — Johnny, Cathy, and Ali.

Noa reached a sharp turn in the path and found the way before her suddenly dark and deserted, much as it must have been when Wendell had been attacked. Noa heard a sound, like stealthy footsteps echoing behind her. Johnny!

Her heart raced with sudden fear. He had definitely not liked her coming to Ali's shop, asking questions and finding him there. Was he thinking she had evidence to prove his involvement? Then she was in danger!

She shot a glance back over her shoulder. A large, shadowy figure slipped back into the gathering darkness of the narrow alley.

Panic exploded in Noa's chest. All the terror of the medina she had felt as a child, plus all the fear she had been suppressing, burst forth like a sudden explosion. Memories of grasping hands and locked walls, of darkness descending, quickened her steps as she ran down one dark passage, then another. Mud-colored walls and long, narrow streets twisted and turned before her without beginning or end, forming one giant, frightening maze. When the ache in her side finally forced Noa to slow down, she looked back again. She had managed to lose whoever had been following her. But now she was utterly, hopelessly lost herself!

Lost in the medina — her greatest fear had become reality. Holding back tears, Noa looked helplessly around her, searching for familiar signs. Noa remembered telling the tour group this morning how one could walk for hours and see only a small portion of the walled city. Her own words now seemed to mock her. How would she ever find her way out of here?

"Does this lead outside?" she asked a Moroccan woman. The woman's dark eyes met

Noa's curiously above the veil, then she turned shyly away. Noa would keep trying to find someone who spoke English. Until then, she would continue walking. Noa chose the wide path to her left. Not knowing where the passage led, she could only hope that it would take her to closer to the city gates.

Noa walked until her legs began to ache from sheer exhaustion. As she turned the corner, the eerie sound of chanting filled the air. From the minaret, the muezzins were calling the faithful to evening prayer. Noa could see clearly the ornate designs upon the tall, thin minaret. The nearness of the building told her that instead of moving toward the entrance, she had been steadily working her way deeper and deeper into the heart of the medina.

Standing beneath the shadow of the minaret, Noa felt like a child again. Through a haze of tears, she chose another path and began to walk.

"You're going the wrong way, Noa."

Noa turned, startled to see Taber only a few steps away from her. His tall form separated him from the crowd as he moved toward her.

Wendell's suspicions of him jumped to mind, but she was still grateful to see him.

"What — what are you doing here?" She wondered if he had been the one following her from Ali's shop. "Were you looking for me?"

He came closer, his smile amused. "No, but I'm glad I found you — in the last place I'd expect you to be. I've always had the impression that the medina frightens you."

"I was lost here once as a child." Noa wondered why she could tell Taber so easily about the terrifying experience she had never before shared with anyone. "And now I'm lost again."

The amusement left his face. His dark eyes studied her with kindness.

"Just show me the way out of here!" She attempted a smile, hoping he could not tell that she had been on the verge of tears.

"I know many shortcuts." A protective hand drew her close to him, making her feel safe. "We'll be at the gates in no time. Now, why are you here alone?"

"I came down here to talk to Ali Balsam."

"Definitely nothing I would have recommended. Did you find out anything?"

"Johnny Ramos was in the shop. I think Ali's the fence, but Johnny's the one who attacked Wendell." Pain caught in her voice as she added, "I'm afraid they are both partners of Cathy's."

"Noa! You can't really believe that!"

"Read this." She drew Mike's letter from her purse and handed it to him.

Lines of concentration deepened along his brow as he studied the words. When he was finished, he handed the letter back to her. "This is a different type of crime than stealing from a father. I don't believe she has anything to do with what's happening here."

Anyone capable of deceiving a man like Mike could certainly do this. Noa stole a look at Taber, unable to understand his confidence in Cathy's innocence. Did he know something she didn't? She wished she hadn't shown him the letter, meant only for her. "Are the police still at the hotel?" she asked.

"Yes. I've already filled out most of the necessary reports on the missing jewel. Of course they'll probably want to talk to you."

"How is Belda taking the loss of her ring?"

"Exceptionally well. In fact, she insists that we go on with the tour."

"I was afraid the police might detain us."

"They have our schedule so they can contact us if they need to. We are free to be on our way to Marrakesh tomorrow." Taber's smile lightened Noa's mood. "That's where I teach you to ride a camel."

Chapter Nine

Noa, her fingers laced in Taber's strong grip, was being led forward toward a man in white, who was wearing a dark blue turban with a scarf looped around his neck. Around him grazed five camels. Near Noa stood an unsaddled one, a gristly, ugly animal with a single, very high hump. Noa stopped and reached out to him cautiously. The camel's neck had shed, leaving bald, bare skin, but a thick, shaggy fur remained on his back. Wild hairlike masses of fur puffed out under his chin and on the crown of his heavy head. "I'd rather go horseback riding," Noa said a little wistfully.

Slender, white Arabian horses and a handsome desert sheik! Now, that would be exciting! More what she had in mind. This mean, awkward beast with thick lips moving ever so slowly had no part in her dream. She cast a glance at Taber. At least he definitely qualified as a sheik!

His white shirt, opened at the throat, revealed thick, black hair. The tight clothing made him seem leaner, more muscular. His smile showed teeth as white as the shirt he wore, contrasting dramatically with his olive skin.

When Taber said, "Better put on that hat," she admitted to herself the uselessness of trying to talk him out of this camel ride into the desert.

Obediently she adjusted the straw hat that dangled from a ribbon across her back. With a long stick, the attendant prodded one of the camels to kneel. The saddle was covered with a woven red blanket. Attached to it was a circular hoop, which she clung to as she mounted. Taber stood close by as the long-legged camel with slow, jarring motions arose to a startling height. "Where are we going?" she asked anxiously.

"Not far. About a mile and a half straight south." Amusement showed by a tightening of his lips, though he spared her the smile. "You'll survive."

Taber caught the bridle rope, keeping it tight in hand as he rose easily onto his camel. He stopped to say something in Arabic to the owner, to put in his hand a sum that brought forth a huge smile. Then he moved ahead as far as the long rope allowed, looking back now and then to shout encouragement.

The stubborn animal Noa rode apparently preferred to remain near the patch of grass stacked beside his owner. Taber urged him to move.

The camel, deciding all at once to go along with Taber, loped forward with a speed that made Noa think she would fall. She leaned toward the skinny neck, both hands grasping the metal loop.

The sky seemed filled with a giant sun that penetrated her straw hat, beat down upon her back, and caused her blouse to stick tight against her skin. "Where are we going?" she asked again. "To an oasis, I hope!"

"To my kasbah! Like the king, I have a palace in each of the four imperial cities — plus Tangier," he added. "I feel as if I am dragging you along." He skillfully shifted the rope, drawing her camel so close to his side that their legs touched.

Noa could not help noticing how very straight he sat, how adept he was at controlling the willful animals. "Why did I ever suggest Arabian horses?" Noa said with some sarcasm. "This is so much fun!"

As if in answer, Taber pulled a camera from his pocket and snapped a shot of her. If the lens was able to capture a picture of such a jogging subject, it would certainly be a horrible one! Noa's damp hair was strung around her face, and her eyes squinted from the light reflected off bright, glistening sand.

Taber snapped another picture. "My scrapbook full of Noa's first journey into the Sahara! That is going to be very valuable to me!"

Straight ahead rose bare, sandy hills, which looked higher from a distance than they did at close range. Between two slopes grew three palm trees, one looming twice as high as the others. Behind them Noa spotted a white house, low and sprawling.

They headed directly to it. At the trees Taber slipped to the ground and caught Noa in his arms. Once her feet were on the sandy earth, he pulled her close, the quick brush of his lips surprising her. Feeling their brief, electric touch gave her the inclination, but not the time, to respond. Taber moved away quickly, his hand tight around hers, as he led her to the doorway.

Because she had such a powerful attraction to him, it was not wise to be alone with him. She actually knew so little about him. He was Thomas Rand's son, but that, according to Wendell, was in itself cause for second thoughts. If Taber could afford mansions like this one, why would he want to work for Carlson-Rand Tours?

"This is magnificent," Noa remarked. "I guess the rumors that you are bankrupt haven't much credibility."

"So the talk of Tangier has reached your lovely ears," Taber said. "It's true I've had some reverses there, but luckily I have holdings elsewhere."

"Do you really own so many homes?"

"Yes. Also," he added teasingly, "I have gold in sunken ships in the Mediterranean. I have treasures hidden under rocks."

His mention of rocks made Noa think of the small square inside the medina at Fez where Wendell had almost been killed. She saw clearly the loose stones set in the columns of the fountain there. It suddenly occurred to her why the police had found no weapon: The attacker had taken the time to set the stone back into the fountain! She didn't know whether fingerprints could be taken from stone, but at least when he had attacked Belda, the thief had worn no gloves. The very minute she returned to Fez, she would check the rocks of the fountain. She felt certain she would find one of them stained with Wendell's blood!

"This is not a monastery," Taber said with

176

a smile. "You don't have to begin deep meditation." He smiled at her as they passed into a patio where lush plants hung from the ceiling and were set in great pots on the tiled floor.

"There's a swimming pool in back," Taber said. "I thought you would like to cool off while I start dinner."

"Dinner?"

"I called ahead and everything this chef needs is here."

His arms encircled her again. She was pressed so close against him she could feel the pounding of his heart. "I hope you don't mind," he said, his lips against her hair. "I dismissed the household so we could be alone!"

This time when he kissed her there was no haste. Gently, slowly, his lips pressed against hers until her feelings overwhelmed her more strongly than ever before. At first she gave into the wonder of it, held him just as tightly as he held her; then, remembering her doubts of him, she struggled to free herself.

Taber gave a quick, low laugh as she slipped away. "My dining room," he said, following her into a dim, cool area with a crudely hewn table surrounded by massive chairs. Beyond it was a room with a pool made entirely of gleaming blue tile.

"How beautiful!" she exclaimed.

"So are you. But no time for romance, I have to cook. We're having our national dish, couscous — chicken, raisins — my specialty." As he spoke he wandered into the pool area and from a wardrobe lifted a swimsuit, which he offered to her. "I never guess wrong about sizes. There's a bedroom to the right where you can change. I'll join you in a little while."

Tired and sweaty from the smolderingly hot sun, and with the camel's smell still clinging to her, she could not resist the call of the cool water. In spite of her better judgment, Noa slipped into the deep red swimsuit. It did fit perfectly. The color had to have been selected to accent her tawny hair. Had he ordered it, the way he had ordered the groceries, as part of a careful plan?

Noa dived into the water. She felt comforted by the coolness of the contact and lulled from her apprehension. She swam the length of the pool and back, returned to the shallow side, and stood up, water streaming from her hair. For a moment amid the dazzling beauty she felt relaxed and strangely happy.

At last, thinking she should help Taber with the meal, she found a towel on a chair beside the pool and dried her hair. Back in the bedroom where she had changed, Noa found a velvet robe that was no doubt Taber's. She saw by the great mirror beside the bed how badly tangled her hair had become while drying. When she opened a drawer to look for a brush, her eyes fell upon a picture frame that lay face down, as if someone had hastily removed it from the dresser.

Forewarned by a sense of awful dread, she lifted the frame. She turned it around slowly and stared at the three faces in the picture, a slight dizziness replacing her recent contentment. She was looking at a picture of Taber, smiling, handsome. Beside him was a beautiful, dark woman, her arm encircling a small, wide-eyed boy. The little boy, three or four years old, looked exactly like Taber!

Noa recalled how rapidly she had dismissed Ali Balsam's explicit reference to Taber's wife! A clear enough warning — one she had put aside without another thought — how stupid! Belda's words rang in her ears: *They have wives all over the place!*

Her momentary feeling of illness was replaced by anger so intense that it affected her vision, caused the picture to become hazy and unclear. Her anger was mingled with hurt, as if she had been stabbed in the stomach with a Moroccan dagger. Married! How could Taber do this to her?

Of course he was married! Why else would he have houses in so many cities?

Noa's anger turned to rage. She wanted to confront him, to do him some physical harm that would make him realize what his deceit had done to her! Instead she struggled into her jeans and blouse and slipped swiftly, quietly into the dining area, now filled with a fragrant smell of spices.

Outside, the camel waited under the palm trees. He ignored her hurried approach, remaining stubbornly motionless except for a slight movement of his mouth. She would never be able to get him to stand, let alone persuade him to take her back to Marrakesh!

What of it? She would rather walk anyway!

Walking in the blazing sun cooled Noa's anger. By the time Taber's house was out of sight, she was beginning to wonder if she should have at least told him that she was leaving. He would have missed her by now.

A cloud of dust covered the empty roadway, and Noa had visions of Taber coming after her, sweeping her off her feet and taking her back to the house. In spite of logic, a part of her wished that he would. Why hadn't she had the courage to confront him with the picture? Had she been afraid he would convince her that no matter how many wives he had, she was the one that belonged in his arms?

The thought of his kiss made her melt like ice cream in the hot sunlight. Taber was not only married, but had probably received the money his father had stolen from Carlson-Rand Tours! Moreover, he might very well be involved in the robbery of Belda's ring. Noa wanted no relationship with a polygamous thief, no matter how handsome and enticing he could be!

The cloud of dust became a visible object, a Berber farmer and two daughters taking rugs to market in an old wagon. With gestures that needed no words, he offered her a ride. She accepted, climbing into the back of the wagon to sit upon the rugs with two shyly smiling girls, their hands and faces dotted with black ink designs in traditional Berber fashion.

The slow, jarring movement of the ancient wagon still seemed preferable to the back of the camel. She gazed toward the Atlas Mountains across the pinkish glare of sand and tried not to think of Taber. In no time, the serrated, rose-colored walls of Marrakesh appeared. The farmer stopped at the edge of the square, letting Noa out only a short distance away from where Taber had rented the camels. She thanked him in English and he waved in an exaggerated, American fashion.

Noa moved reluctantly into the bizarre gathering of snake charmers, acrobats, and organ-grinders, which made up the famous Marrakesh square. At first she was pleased with its fairy-tale quality, how it looked like a circus set beneath desert sun, but as she advanced, she felt enclosed and a little threatened.

Through the jostling crowd, Noa suddenly spotted Greg and Cathy, their heads bent together as if immersed in serious conversation. She gratefully edged forward to join them where they had stopped in front of a snake charmer.

"Noa! I didn't expect to see you here," Greg said. "I was just trying to talk Cathy into getting her picture taken with that snake."

"No way!" Cathy protested. "I hate snakes!" For all her reluctance, she seemed definitely tempted. Noa saw the curious look in her eyes as the snake charmer lifted the smaller of the snakes from a basket at his feet and held it out to her. Of course Cathy would be fascinated by any suggestion of danger. "What if it bites me?"

"I'll bet Noa a dollar that you don't have the guts to do it!" Greg said with a laugh.

"You're on!" Noa said, trying to catch their playful spirit. "My niece is the bravest girl in Morocco! She wouldn't be bothered by any poisonous cobra."

Cathy took a deep breath and shuddered. Silver bracelets jingled on her wrists as she raised one arm. "All right, I'll do it! But please, Greg. Take the picture fast!"

With a gap-toothed smile, the gaunt, dark-skinned man in his white robes draped the snake over Cathy's shoulders, which were bare except for the thin straps of her halter top. "Ooh, I hate you guys for this! Cold and slimy and — awful!" Cathy closed her eyes, opening them just long enough for Greg to snap his picture. But when the old man removed the snake, she was smiling.

"See, that wasn't so bad, was it?" Greg teased.

"I'm willing to try anything once!" Cathy said, hugging her bare shoulders where the snake had touched them. "I just can't get that creepy feeling off me. I feel like he's still there, wrapped around my neck. Let's go back to the hotel for a swim!"

"I just got here," Greg said.

"I've been walking around for hours. I'm hot and my skin feels creepy. I'm going back."

"I'll go with you," Noa volunteered.

"I can find my way."

"Let her go. She'll be fine," Greg interceded. "She got down here on her own."

As Cathy disappeared into the crowd, Noa asked, "Where did you meet up with her?"

"That's a great story in itself." Greg pointed to some women selling the kind of bracelets Cathy wore. "I had to rescue her from that pack!"

"This is the first time I've seen women in Morocco out selling."

"If you call that selling. One of the women told Cathy the bracelets were a gift, put them on her arm, and then demanded payment. She wouldn't take them back and wouldn't let Cathy go until she paid her something for them. They were yelling and screaming at each other! Cathy didn't have any money, so I had to bail her out."

"Let me pay for the bracelets."

"The cost was nothing. The excitement was enough to last all day." As they continued to walk, Greg pulled out a guidebook. "They call this square 'd Jemma el Fna.' The

'Streets of the Dead' or the 'Concourse of Sinners.' "

"This is nice, having someone else giving the information for once," Noa said. "Why do they call it the 'Streets of the Dead'?"

"At one time criminals were executed here, and their heads were impaled on stakes at the corners of the square."

"I think I prefer the other name, 'Concourse of Sinners.' "

Greg glanced at the motley crowd surrounding them. "That would fit better. I'd hate to be alone here at night. This place must be swarming with pickpockets!"

Noa hurried to keep up with him, agreeing that the square, despite its carnivallike atmosphere, seemed evil and grasping. She imagined that drugs were offered in the same variety and abundance as were the trinkets. Their quick pace caused the vendors that followed them to lag behind them, but she could still feel cold, watching eyes.

The merciless heat, as well as having missed a meal, made Noa feel a little dizzy and light-headed. She was grateful when Greg announced that he was hungry. Once again, he opened his handy little guidebook. "The sidewalk café down the street has three stars." A smile lit the corners of his mouth. "I guess that means we can get a sandwich without having to worry about food poisoning."

Crowds passed in front of the huge café window where they sat so they could watch the busy street, and see the terra-cotta walls and brilliant summer flowers. Blue, gold, and red glittered everywhere. A fantasia soldier, dressed in formal costume, passed by on his proud Arabian horse. With a pang Noa remembered Taber, who had managed somehow to look twice as elegant astride a camel.

Their roast beef sandwiches came with packaged potato chips and bottled pop. The bread was crusty and dry. Greg watched Noa with clear, blue-green eyes. His skin had tanned from many swims in hotel pools; tiny golden lights rippled through his crisp brown hair. Noa thought of Belda's advice — that she should welcome Greg's attention, and forget Taber.

"I hope you've had a nice vacation, despite all the trouble we've had," Noa said.

"Having you as a guide has made it all worthwhile." He reached across the table and took her hand in his. "In fact, I was hoping maybe you will fly out to Newark. I'll give you a tour of the college."

She thought of Wendell's investigation

and the fact that Greg had never enrolled. "It's an engineering school, isn't it?"

"Yes."

"How long have you been enrolled there?"

"One year," he answered promptly. He must have read the doubt or accusation in her glance, for when he spoke again, he seemed embarrassed. "I don't know why I ever told you that. I haven't actually enrolled yet. But I'm going to!" His eyes shifted to the table, then lifted to hers. "I wasn't really lying. I was only projecting what will soon be a reality. I guess I was just trying to impress you. I didn't think you'd be interested in a day laborer." Greg's hand tightened around hers. "That's okay, isn't it?"

Noa laughed, "When I know about it, it is."

"Look! There's Taber! Maybe he'll join us." Greg waved his free hand back and forth to attract Taber's attention.

Taber had drawn to a stop a few feet in front of the huge window. Noa hoped he would not look around and see Greg and her. He would surely misunderstand.

Taber looked up and down the street, straightened, then turned. His dark eyes gazed directly into hers, then dropped to

Greg's fingers so possessively entwined in her own.

The black brows knit and his lips compressed as disbelief shadowed his face — disbelief which blackened into a smoldering disdain.

"What's wrong with him?" Greg asked her, as Taber turned on his heel and rapidly vanished into the crowd.

Chapter Ten

When Noa thought of Taber, it had become a habit to picture him standing by Johnny inside the bus, his dark eyes glowing as he spoke, one arm overhead braced against the constantly swaying vehicle. Noa allowed her eyes to stray toward him now; she was disquieted by the edge to his voice, and the remoteness in his sharp features made him seem like a stranger.

Beside her Greg stirred uncomfortably. Noa turned to stare out the window at dry, dusty fields interspersed with the mud huts of Berber villages. From Casablanca the tour would return to Fez, then come full circle back to Tangier. There it would end.

She could not shut out Taber's voice. "In about two hours we'll arrive in Casablanca." His tone had become dry, mocking, as he added, "The city of romance."

"Here's looking at you, kid!" Belda

jammed an elbow into Milton's stomach.

Everyone laughed.

"I see we have some Humphrey Bogart fans."

"Who's Bogart?" Cathy demanded.

"No one's *that* young!" Belda exclaimed. She had not let the loss of the ring infringe upon her good time.

"You've surely seen *Casablanca* on TV." Greg looked around to question Cathy, who sat with Orva. The other girls from the school were seated in the back with Marie.

"The movie wasn't filmed in Casablanca," Noa said automatically. "In fact, it's never even been shown there."

"You're trying to spoil all the romance," Greg teased.

Belda, across the aisle from them, looked directly at Greg. "Wouldn't it be the greatest place on earth to propose to the one you love?"

"If a struggling student had the resources to marry, I'd be tempted to ask someone," Greg replied seriously.

"Never let money, or the lack of it, get in the way of love!" Belda glanced pointedly from Greg to Noa.

Noa responded by looking out of the window again. Because of Belda, everyone was beginning to think of Greg and her as a couple. Let them think whatever they liked. Noa had no dreams at all of romance. For her, no Humphrey Bogart waited by the seashore in Casablanca — no Taber Rand!

Taber had returned the microphone to the rack and seated himself. His profile exaggerated his tense jaw, which made him seem angry.

Greg's arm moved along the back of the seat until his hand touched Noa's shoulder. "I've always said I'll marry for love or not at all!"

"Oh, yes." Belda's sharp hearing missed nothing. "Love!" She poked the snoring Milton again with her elbow. "How lucky you are, Noa. Your man's awake!"

Belda's comments had begun to annoy Noa. Why did she persist in encouraging Greg? Noa's thoughts drifted to the tour's start and how happy Taber and she had been then. Loss of trust had brought loss of . . . everything. Taber had been right — love and trust must be one.

Greg's hand tightened on Noa's shoulder. Noa glanced back and caught Cathy watching them. Her yellowish eyes had narrowed. Noa thought for a moment of Greg and Cathy walking so close together through the square at Marrakesh. Could

Cathy, despite the fact that she usually ig-nored Greg, really like him? Or was Cathy just resentful because she thought the two of them were very happy?

To block out Taber's anger and Cathy's sullen face, Noa rested her head against the seat and closed her eyes. She must have dozed, for when she opened her eyes again, Taber was speaking into the microphone. "I wholeheartedly recommend a swim in the ocean. The afternoon tour doesn't begin until three this afternoon. That gives you plenty of time."

A long strip of golden sand crammed with striped umbrellas lay just beyond the sprawling resort. "As soon as I get my lug-gage, I'm going straight down to the beach!" Noa heard Cathy say to Orva.

"A swim does sound great!" Greg said as they stepped from the bus. "Let's join the girls, Noa!"

Noa wished she could feel enthusiasm in-stead of great weariness. "Why don't you go on ahead? I'll meet you there later."

Noa could stand on the balcony of her room and look toward the glistening blue of the water. The sight of the gentle waves and brilliant clouds served only to deepen her sadness. Even the thought of swimming, which she usually enjoyed, sounded like some dreary chore.

Some time later she managed to convince herself that no matter how she felt, she should try to fulfill her job and participate in the activities. As she started slowly toward the beach, she saw Cathy in a skimpy bikini swimming with Orva and several of the other schoolgirls. Noa was relieved to see her finally accepted as a part of their group.

Greg lay on a towel very near the water. The relaxed position made him look thinner and more boyish, like Huck Finn on his Mississippi raft. She sank down beside him. "You look comfortable," she said.

Greg rolled from his back onto his stomach. Bracing his hands under his chin, he said with a sigh, "Ahh — this is heaven!" He grinned up at Noa. "I wish I had something to drink, but I'm too lazy to go after anything."

"I'll get us some Cokes."

"Thanks, Noa. There's some change in my cap."

Warm sand sifted through her bare toes as Noa walked back up the beach toward the soft-drink machine she had seen earlier. The process darkened her spirits even more, making her think of the walk on the beach Taber and she had taken in Tangier. Cokes in hand, she started back to Greg.

"Noa." The sharp voice startled her, caused her eyes to rise suddenly from the gleaming sand. Taber had stepped directly into her path and was looming above her, prohibiting her escape.

White swim trunks contrasted with the tanned, muscular body. His chest was covered with curling black hair that glistened with ocean water.

Noa's grip tightened on the Cokes and she felt awkward and slightly threatened.

"For me? Thanks." With a spark of devilment in his eyes, Taber took one of the cans from her and took a long drink from Greg's Coke. The boldness of the act rendered Noa speechless. "You missed a delicious dinner yesterday. I had such a great time trying to decide which carefully prepared dish was the best."

If he thought he was going to make her feel guilty, he was mistaken. It was he, not she, who should feel remorse. Noa started around him, but Taber's lean hand locked on her arm. "Let's talk," he said, escorting her to one of the beach tables.

Beneath the shade of a striped umbrella he studied her, the smile she liked so well making little crinkles around his eyes. "I think I've finally figured out what's wrong with you."

"There's nothing wrong with me." Noa stole a glance toward the beach where Greg still lay sunning himself.

"Noa, I'm not married."

Noa stared down at the white table in front of her to avoid looking into Taber's eyes. She could almost see reflected there an image of the Moroccan woman and the boy with the great dark eyes. They had to belong to him. He had to be lying!

"Did you see something there at the house to make you think I was married? Maybe some of Aysha's clothes?"

"Who is Aysha?"

He laughed a little. "So that's it! Aysha is my sister. She has a boy named Thomas."

"I saw a picture of you, a beautiful woman, and a boy who looks exactly like you."

"She is not my wife, Noa. I swear it! I never dreamed you would think otherwise."

Noa studied his dark, serious eyes, the lips compressed in anxious concern. Did she dare accept so simple an explanation? How much she wanted to believe him! Hope battled with reason, only to be defeated by one final bit of information. "Ali Balsam said you were in his shop last month buying a gift — for your wife."

"The necklace was for Aysha's birthday.

We're very close, I always bring her and Thomas presents when I go through Fez." The smile deepened. "When I told Ali the sapphires were for a beautiful woman, he must have jumped to his own conclusions.

Did she dare trust him? Looking into his eyes right now, she could easily let herself be convinced!

"Believe me, Noa." Taber's hand closed over hers. "I have no wives hidden away. Not even a girlfriend!"

He wasn't married! Noa felt a sense of joy, of relief. "My sister was raised by our mother, so she is of the Moslem faith. But my father, who raised me, was Protestant through and through. If I marry, it will be to one woman, and for life."

The way he was looking at her, as if she might be that woman, made Noa's heart burst with happiness. She glanced at the Coke in Taber's hand and was suddenly reminded of Greg, still waiting for her on the beach.

Guiltily she looked again toward the ocean. Greg still had not moved from his beach towel near the water's edge. But Cathy was hurrying up the beach toward them. A scowl that warned of trouble darkened her face.

Noa drew her hand away from Taber's. "I

think Cathy wants to talk to me," she said, rising.

"Just a minute." Taber returned with a Coke. "Don't forget to take this to your boyfriend," he said, pressing the drink into her hand with a smile.

Noa started toward Cathy. "Were you looking for me?"

Cathy stopped a few feet from her, but craned her neck to see around Noa. "Who were you with?"

Noa glanced back in the direction Cathy looked, but Taber was out of sight. She answered with a question of her own. "What do you want?"

"Do I ever get anything I want from you?"

"What's wrong with you now?"

Cathy's frown deepened. "How long are we going to go on like this?"

"I don't know what you mean."

"I mean with you treating me like a peasant!"

Noa said nothing.

"I'm Mike's daughter! Remember?" Her voice filled with anguish. "I don't know why he left me out! Why did he leave everything to you when I'm his daughter?"

Noa had learned from experience that trying to reason with Cathy was impossible. Again she remained silent.

"Are you going to divide Mike's money with me or not?"

"Not in the near future. That wouldn't be Mike's wish."

"When I'm eighteen?"

"Probably not even then. I expect you to go on to college. The money is a decision we will make later."

"That's not fair! I won't get any of it! I'll just never get away from you!"

"You shouldn't want to. I'm Mike's sister and your friend."

Cathy looked around again. Sunlight caused the flecks of yellow to make her seem very wild or very frightened. "You act worse than I do — flirting with everyone all the time!" Her voice rose, seeming less angry than hysterical. "Something is going to happen to you, Noa! If you're not careful — and you're not!"

Cathy — concerned about her? Surely this was some kind of joke, a ploy on Cathy's part to gain another of her selfish ends.

Noa started to answer, but was startled into silence by the real fear she read in Cathy's eyes. Was the girl trying to warn her about something — about someone? Beads of sweat mixed with the moisture from the cans of Coke she held. Automatically Noa's gaze shifted from her niece to the path Taber had taken.

"What are you trying to tell me?" She turned back to address the empty space where Cathy had stood. Cathy was running away. The movements of her strong body were swift. She was already passing by the group of girls who called to her from the water.

Despite the warm sunlight, Noa shivered a little inside. For an instant she wondered if Cathy's words to her had been intended as a warning — or a threat.

Once in her room, Noa pinned up her damp hair and changed into a white cotton dress. Feeling a strong urge to talk to someone she knew really cared about her, she put through a call to the hospital at Fez where Wendell was still staying.

A sense of shock filled her as the desk clerk replied in broken English, "Mr. Carlson is no longer here."

"Has he been released so soon?"

"He checked himself out a few hours ago."

"How may I reach him?"

"He left no messages for anyone."

Dismayed and puzzled, Noa hung up the phone. Surely Wendell wouldn't leave the hospital without contacting anyone. So many people depended upon him. In all the years she had known him, he had never failed to leave a forwarding number. What did this mean?

Without direction from her conscious mind, this question merged with a series of events: the attack on Wendell in the medina when he should have been on his way to the bank, Johnny's unexpected appearance at Ali's shop, Taber's finding her — or following her. A feeling that the whole thing was a conspiracy smothered her. At this very moment, Ali Balsam was no doubt selling Belda's ring on the black market.

What if Carlson-Rand Tours was a front for black-market activities?

But Wendell just couldn't be involved — she had known and trusted him for too many years to believe that! If Carlson-Rand Tours were implicated, it would be because of Thomas Rand and the fact that his dealings were being continued by his son, Taber, and whomever Taber had engaged to work for him!

The phone rang shrilly. Taber's voice sounded crisp and somewhat worried. "Noa, you're going to have to handle the city tour alone. Something has come up that can't wait. I'm not going to be able to make it."

She answered cautiously. "Is there something I can help you with?"

"You can help me most by taking care of the tour." He paused. "There's nothing to worry about. Johnny knows Casablanca like the back of his hand. A local guide will be waiting for you at the Royal Palace. Don't forget, the tour today doesn't include lunch. You can stop near the ocean where there's a choice of small cafés."

"I'll get along all right." After a short pause, Noa added, "Taber, has Wendell contacted you?"

"Wendell? No."

"I called the hospital a few hours ago. Wendell is no longer there."

"That's odd. The doctor told me he wouldn't be released for several more days."

"He wasn't released. He just left, early this morning. I'm worried about him."

"There's nothing to worry about. I'm sure Carlson can take care of himself."

"He's never done anything like this before. He likes knowing people can reach him."

A thoughtful silence followed. "I'll see what I can find out. I'll meet you for dinner right after the tour. Why don't you come right down to the dining room? I'll reserve a private table away from the group, so we can talk."

Heartened by the promise, Noa hung up and glanced at her watch. She must hurry or she would be late meeting with the group.

On the way down she paused to tap at Cathy's door. "Cathy. Time for the tour."

Cathy opened the door a crack. "I'm not going," she said. "I don't feel good. My shoulders and back really hurt." She moaned a little. "Too much African sun!"

Noa, who always tanned easily, hadn't thought of the possibility of fair-skinned Cathy's being sunburned. "I hope you don't blister," she said, feeling a little guilty that she hadn't warned her to take precautions. "Maybe I should take a look at your shoulders."

The loose, striped kaftan Cathy had thrown on over her swimsuit reminded Noa of one she had seen Taber wear several times. Of course, they all looked alike to her.

"I put some lotion on," Cathy said hurriedly. "I'll be fine."

The kaftan swirled about Cathy's bare feet as she firmly closed the door.

Chapter Eleven

Always punctual, the entire group, with the exception of Cathy and Taber, were waiting in the lobby. "Where's Taber?" Moulay Aziz asked, missing him first.

As Noa explained that he was not going along with them, she saw Marie scan the group the way teachers do when mentally calling roll. "Your niece isn't joining us either?" she asked with raised brow.

With a tightness in her throat, Noa explained about the sunburn. Was Marie thinking what she had been thinking? That Taber's absence and Cathy's had some connection?

"I hope we're not going to another medina today," Milton complained. He had grown increasingly difficult since his argument with the police in Fez. He resented not only the loss of the precious ring, but also the fact that the authorities had actually dared to consider him a suspect.

"Another day, another medina," Belda chirped, trying to placate him with one of Taber's jokes.

"Isn't there anything else in Morocco to see?"

"As a matter of fact, we have something entirely different planned for today," Noa said. "No medina. We're going to drive out along the seacoast, drive by the site where the historic conference of Allied leaders took place during World War II, and make a stop at the Royal Palace.

"That'll be interesting, won't it, Milton?" Belda said, giving him a nudge.

"Are we going to stop at Rick's Café?" Greg asked with a smile.

"As I mentioned before, the movie *Casablanca* wasn't actually filmed here. If there *is* a Rick's Café, I'm afraid it's a phony."

"Noa, I remember Rick's from my last trip here," Belda said. "It's right near the palace. They have the best tea — and a piano bar! We can still stop there, can't we?"

"I don't see why not, since it's on the way."

Out of the corner of her eye, Noa saw Johnny pulling up in the space across the street from the hotel. She tried to sound happy as she called, "All aboard!"

As Belda started to lead the way out of the

hotel, Milton called her back, with, Noa noticed, a slight edge to his voice. "Belda, dear. Don't forget your purse. You've left it on the sofa."

"Oh, I'm getting so darned absent-minded," she said as Milton brought the huge white leather bag to her. "Thank you, Miltie."

"I have to watch her every minute," Milton grumbled. "She'd forget her head if it wasn't fastened on." Milton's words held a sting despite the humorous delivery. His eyes, as they fastened on Noa, held an unspoken accusation. She knew he blamed both Belda and her for the missing ring.

"I'm not the one who left my razor and shaving cream at the last hotel!" Belda snapped at him. Her sharp remark left Milton without retaliation, silently stroking the five-o'clock shadow upon his coarse face.

Cars and buses whizzed by on the congested street that ran past the hotel. "Be careful crossing the street," Noa cautioned the group. "We're in the big city now."

Greg, with great chivalry, helped Noa get the group across safely. "Whew! The Moroccans don't pay much attention to a crosswalk sign, do they?"

Noa laughed. "Casablanca has over three

million people. And we're used to dodging donkeys, not automobiles!"

Compared to the African wildness of Marrakesh, Casablanca seemed tame, civilized. New buildings, hotels, and skyscrapers gleamed white in the afternoon sun. No danger here. Noa was glad she was in a modern city again, where she felt safe.

"Four hundred kinds of flowers grow here," Noa said as they drove through the residential sections, stopping at the site of the famous meeting of the Allied leaders. She spoke of Churchill and Roosevelt. "The original hotel is gone now, but another has sprung up in its spot."

The bus drove along the seacoast to view the ships, then stopped in front of the Royal Palace with its buff-colored walls and green tile roof. Two armed guards in full uniform stood near the door. True to Taber's word, a husky, African man in a jellaba and red tarboosh was waiting to greet the tour bus. "The King won't allow tours inside," Noa explained. "But the guide will take us around the grounds."

The group gathered near the huge stone pavilion that surrounded the palace. The guide began to tell of the history behind the palace.

Grateful that the guide had taken over,

Noa rested her arm against a huge, rusty cannon that still pointed outward from the wall as if to protect the immense stone palace from intruders.

Lost in thought, she looked out at the white-topped buildings of the town visible from the rise of the hill. She heard the sound of footsteps moving away from her as the tour group proceeded to the next point of interest. She could hear the guide giving the names of the pink, flowering bushes and leafy green trees that surrounded the great building.

Noa turned abruptly and almost ran into Marie, who still stood close by, a tall, angular figure in her trim jacket and shapeless brown skirt. The blowing wind that whipped Noa's hair around her face did not make a ripple in Marie's stiff, darkish blond curls.

Without introduction, Marie said what was on her mind. "You probably know by now that we were wrong about who Cathy was with the other night," she said, unsmiling. "It's Taber, not Johnny, that Cathy has been sneaking out to meet all along."

Unnerved at hearing her own suspicions being voiced aloud by someone else, Noa asked, "What makes you think that?"

"I caught them together late last night.

Cathy tried to duck around the corridor when she saw me, but I knew it was her. Taber had his arm around her. They had just left his room."

A vision of the kaftan Cathy wore this afternoon, so much like Taber's, leaped to Noa's mind. The image made her ill, made Marie's world-hardened face grow distant and obscure. Taber and Cathy — involved! Cathy, so very young! "Are you sure you're not mistaken?"

"Where are Cathy and Taber this afternoon?" As if their mutual absence was proof enough of their guilt, Marie tossed back her head and moved briskly away from Noa. At that moment, Noa disliked her intensely, hated the artificial tint of her hair, the way she walked so tall and straight. Why should she spy on Cathy and Taber?

Noa wanted to believe that Marie was purposefully trying to cause trouble for Taber. It was much more likely that Marie and Wendell were involved than Taber and Cathy!

She remembered the gambling trips and vacations with Wendell that Marie had spoken of; they were obviously much closer than Wendell had ever let on. Wasn't it even likely that Wendell and Marie . . . ?

Noa remembered her first meeting with

Marie on the boat to Tangier. Even then, she had been looking for Wendell. Together, she and Wendell might have plotted the theft of the jewel down to the last detail before the tour had ever begun.

The jewel was gone. And now Wendell had disappeared from the hospital without a trace.

Firmly Noa checked her runaway thoughts. Marie was only trying to help her, and Wendell was the dearest, kindest person she had ever known, as much a part of her family as her brother, Mike.

Rick's Café was worse than a phony, with its glitzy piano bar and blown-up posters of Humphrey Bogart and Ingrid Bergman. The artificiality of the atmosphere would have made Noa laugh if Greg and Belda weren't so serious and impressed. They kept exchanging glances, as if they shared some secret.

"We have to sit close to the piano bar," Belda insisted. Greg and Noa sat down at a table. Noa expected Belda and Milton to join them, but they moved off to another table nearby.

"Play it again, Sam," Belda called. The small, dark man at the piano seemed bored, his playing mediocre at best, until Belda came up and placed a fistful of bills from her purse into his bowl. She whispered her request. The little man flashed a big smile at Greg and Noa, then began playing enthusiastically.

Belda stopped by their table, singing in a low voice, "It's still the same old story!" She patted Greg's arm. "The rest is up to you!"

As Belda walked away, Greg grinned. "Belda's loyal to my cause!" he said.

"Your cause?"

"You. The fact that I'm crazy about you!" His clear, blue eyes held hers. Time in the sun had lightened Greg's thick, brown hair, and the blue of his knit shirt accentuated his tan.

"I'm hoping we can see each other after the tour." Gently he took both of her hands in his. "In fact, I want to see you every day for the rest of my life."

"Greg, you're not —"

"Yes, I am," he said shyly. "Like Belda says, who could think of a more romantic place to propose than Casablanca?"

Rick's Café, no less. She watched uneasily as he took a small box from his pocket and handed it to her. Inside was a tiny diamond set in gold.

"Greg, I can't accept this. It's just — too sudden." She felt embarrassed, half afraid to meet his disappointed gaze. Greg — so earnest and handsome. Any woman would be glad for his attention. And yet Noa could not stop herself from wishing that not Greg, but Taber, was here beside her, offering her his ring, a promise of his love. She knew then what her answer would have been.

Once again, Greg stopped to assist Noa in guiding the group across the busy street. "Thanks, Greg. I appreciated your help today."

"Then how about dinner?"

"I'm sorry. I can't."

"Another business meeting?" A ripple of darkness moved through Greg's eyes, making them suddenly appear more green than blue. She could sense his irritation, even a flash of anger as he said, "In a few more days the tour will be over, Noa. I want to spend some time alone with you."

"We'll talk soon. I promise." Greg had taken the rejection of his ring with good-natured optimism. He had even hinted that he might fly out to Algeciras to see Noa before his classes started in the fall. Noa wished she could find some way to discourage him without hurting his feelings. She knew what it was like to be hurt by love. "I have to go, Greg." Noa could sense that he was watching her as she moved quickly away.

As Noa entered the dining room, thoughts of Greg were quickly replaced by images of Taber. She looked around the darkened room for sight of him, but her gaze locked not on Taber's dark eyes, but on eyes that were startlingly light and a little sardonic, surrounded by creases that edged downward to thin, smiling lips. "Wendell! I didn't expect to see you!"

As he rose with a great dignity, amusement lit his face. "I thought I'd surprise you. I just got in. I met Taber in the hallway and he said he was meeting you here. I thought I'd join you, if you don't mind."

"Of course we don't mind!" Despite the bandage that seemed to add to his paleness, he appeared normal. The bruise that darkened his temple had spread downward across his jawline, but it no longer looked ominous. "But you shouldn't have left the hospital. The doctor. . . ."

Wendell's raised hand caused her words to fade away. "I couldn't take another minute of that deadly dullness, so I checked myself out early this morning, rented a car, and drove down here."

She had been so worried about him and all the time he had been on his way to see her! "I'm so glad you're here!" Noa felt relieved and happy as she seated herself across the table from him.

Wendell lifted his briefcase embossed with huge gold letters saying *Carlson-Rand Tours.* He placed before her a stack of papers. "Here is a complete financial statement for the business," he said, "along with a partnership agreement. Informal, of course, but enough for me to go ahead with the contract."

Noa studied the report for a long while. Her voice sounded hesitant to her when she finally spoke. "Nothing to find fault with here. Profits are exceptional."

"When no one tampers with them," Wendell added curtly.

Noa had never noticed this particular tone to his voice. Perhaps Wendell the businessman was not quite the same person as Wendell the friend.

"I'm going to need an answer, Noa. No later than next Saturday, June twenty-fifth."

"Why so soon?"

"If you don't want the partnership, I have someone who does. You, of course, are my first choice."

The provisions of Mike's will gave her complete control of his investments. She could sign now, act at once. She couldn't lose the one thing she had wanted all of her life! Still she hesitated.

Doubtfully Noa read through the agreement he had drawn up. She was aware of his confident waiting, his slight smile when she at last extended her hand for the pen he supplied from his breast pocket. "No need to wait at all," Noa said as she signed the agreement. "I definitely want to be your partner!"

Greatly pleased, Wendell shook hands with her. As Wendell returned the papers to his briefcase, he said, "I've got some news for you, Noa. I told you about Graham's investigation. He's come up with some surprising new evidence concerning the company's missing funds."

"What did he find out?"

"He found out that Thomas Rand was never guilty. He was set up by the head accountant. You probably remember Sam Morrison? He gave a full confession. It makes me feel very good and very bad. If I had only known. . . ."

"It's too late now to look back," Noa said gently.

A tightening of deep lines in Wendell's face expressed a sardonic acceptance, like the shrug of a shoulder. "Too late for me to make it up to Thomas." Wendell's large eyes raised to the doorway Taber had just entered. "But there's still his son. . . ."

"What are you talking about with your heads so close together?" Taber asked, as he seated himself between them. "Me?"

Wendell said with a light chuckle, "I was just praising Noa for the wonderful job you two have done keeping the tour together under such trying circumstances."

"I couldn't have done it without Noa," Taber said.

At the same time, Noa began, "The credit really should go to Taber."

"So you two are willing to share the praise as well as the blame! That's what I call real teamwork!" He paused, beaming appreciation. "Because we've been successful in keeping the . . . unfortunate incident of professional theft out of the news, we already have a full tour booked for July. I'm convinced this Moroccan venture is going to be a big success, after all! I've decided to make it a permanent part of our agenda. And to celebrate — we're all having steak tonight, compliments of Carlson-Rand!"

"I don't believe this," Taber said to Noa. "Are you sure it's in the budget?"

A twinkle appeared in Wendell's eyes, but his voice remained serious. "My friends, for the first time in years Carlson-Rand is in the black again." Wendell lifted his water glass. Vanishing sarcasm left only kindliness as he looked from Taber to Noa. "Let's drink a toast to its remaining that way."

"The three of us make a great trio!" Noa said.

Taber, eyes sparkling, tapped his glass against Noa's. "I'll drink to that!"

Noa had not realized how heavily fear and suspicion had weighed upon her until they were replaced with this glow of happiness and security. Her greatest hopes had been realized! Noa was a full partner in the tour company, and Taber, like his father, had been proven innocent!

Noa's high spirits lasted through a radiant dinner, until she saw Cathy coming toward them. Her hair had grown to almost shoulder length during the trip. The sun had bleached the ends almost white, making the roots appear even darker. The contrast gave her a wild, striking appearance. The strapless blouse and shorts she wore re-vealed smooth, perfectly tanned shoulders and legs. Noa could not see the slightest sign of blister or sunburn. Before she could make any comment, Cathy said in a sing-song voice. "Guess what, Noa? Someone left a purse on the bus!"

"How do you know?"

"I ran into Johnny. He said to tell you it's a big, white purse. He said don't worry — the bus is locked."

From the description Noa knew the purse belonged to Belda. "Thanks for telling me," Noa said, as Cathy bounded away. Noa turned to Taber. "I'd better return Belda's purse to her before she starts to worry. Do you have the keys to the bus with you?"

He shook his head. "Sorry. I left them back in my room. Do you want me to go up and get them?"

"No, I'll just get mine."

Taber rose to accompany her, but Wendell stopped him. "You stay, Taber. I want to talk to you."

When Noa, keys in hand, returned to the lobby, she stopped to glance into the dining room, but both Wendell and Taber were gone. She looked around for them, but they were nowhere in sight.

The setting sun threw slanted rays against the glass doors of the hotel. The harsh glare caused Noa to shield her eyes. Traffic upon the busy street seemed worse than it had been this afternoon. Sure that the way was clear, Noa hurried across the street to where the bus was parked.

Upon the fifth seat, she discovered Belda's leather bag. She took a quick glance inside. She still would not put it past Johnny to pilfer a few bills and credit cards. Satisfied that no one had rummaged through its contents, Noa shouldered the bag, locked the bus, and stood waiting for the traffic to clear.

The steady stream of cars was interrupted by a short break in traffic. With quick steps, Noa started across the street.

Noa had reached the center of the road when a white car turned the corner and recklessly speeded toward her. Instinctively, Noa jumped back. Breathless from her narrow escape, she raced to get out of the street.

Noa heard the squeal of tires behind her as the car made a sudden lunge to the right. Once again, it headed straight toward her! Noa caught a glimpse of the driver. The sight made her blood freeze in her veins. Behind the wheel bent a dark figure swathed in scarf and hooded burnoose.

Tires spun as wheels scraped the edge of the street. A single scream tore from Noa's throat as the car jumped the curb and lurched toward her. She took another step backward, stumbling as her heel struck a rough place in the pavement. She was losing her balance, falling — She could see the bright chrome, the dirty edges of hot, spinning wheels only inches away. She would be crushed beneath them!

"Noa!" Taber' s voice rang out harshly. His arms thrust her forward, ahead of him, away from danger. Behind them, Noa heard an angry squeal of tires being turned back across the curb into the road. She got a fleeting glimpse of the car careening in and out of traffic.

Noa clung to Taber. His arms gathered her closer. She was grateful for their strength, knowing her shaking legs would not have supported her.

"Did you see what happened?" she said, sobbing. "Someone tried to kill me!"

He pulled her even closer. "Did you see who was behind the wheel?"

"No." Noa thought of the figure swathed in heavy disguise and cried against Taber's shoulder.

"Let's get you back inside," he said gently.

A crowd had gathered at the hotel entrance. Inside, curious faces pressed against the glass window. Noa heard Taber telling them that it was nothing, a reckless driver had lost control turning the corner and run up on the curb. No harm done. Noa listened to his calm voice, his careful explanations. Had he believed Noa when she had told him that someone had tried to run her down? Or had he attributed her words to the shock of her close brush with death?

The crowd slowly began dispersing. As they cleared, Noa recognized Moulay Aziz standing in the doorway. He stood very still and rigid, his dark robe blowing with the movement of wind.

Slowly his small, feverishly bright eyes found them. They seemed to look at Taber and her simultaneously as he moved toward them. It was Noa he addressed. "I saw the whole thing," he said, his English a little more broken than usual. "This — what happened — was no accident. Someone deliberately tried to murder you." As his glance shifted to Taber, the slightly out-of-focus eyes seemed to fill with accusation. "I wish to speak with the police."

"Of course. I'll go with you. Noa, you just wait here. You'll be all right, won't you?"

"Yes."

Noa felt the weight of Belda's purse, which still clung by its wide leather straps to her shoulder. She examined it for damage. The large white leather purse that had almost cost her her life seemed unscathed by the incident.

A sick, queasy feeling began in Noa's stomach as she suddenly remembered how Cathy had sent her out there for the purse. Had she used the purse as bait, a lure to get

220

Noa to cross the busy street? Had Cathy been behind the wheel of that car, trying to run her down?

Noa felt a sense of shock. Could the girl hate her that much? The answer seemed painfully clear. Cathy had always stolen for profit, and now she was willing to kill! Noa had no will — if she died, Mike's entire fortune would be legally transferred to her next of kin, to Cathy, to spend on clothes, men, whatever she wanted.

That must be what this whole thing had been about all along. Cathy, so greedy and impatient, wanted Mike's money to spend now. The series of robberies, even the theft of Belda's jewel, were only a sideline, a carefully set-up scheme so that when Noa was killed it would look as though she had been the victim of some professional jewel thief.

Noa remembered the loosened pillar at the ruins. The "accident" had not been meant for Belda at all, but for her. Someone, maybe Johnny, was helping Cathy. She surely must have an accomplice. But even if she did, even if someone else had been behind the wheel, the planning of Noa's "accident" could have originated with no one but Cathy. Only Cathy would benefit from Noa's death!

Chapter Twelve

Usually Noa carried on with her job automatically whether she felt like it or not. She prodded herself to rise, take hold of the overhead luggage rack to steady herself, adjust the microphone, and speak. That wasn't anything she hadn't done hundreds of times before. But right now she couldn't bear facing the thirteen people who sat behind her. Rising would mean looking directly at Cathy.

Taber, who could usually be counted on to interpret her needs and to fill in for her, today stared grimly from the window. Although the seat beside her had been empty, he had sat across the aisle. He avoided looking at her and she, too, avoided giving him any obvious attention. Yet she was aware of the frown cut deeply between his very dark eyes and the tension in the set of his jaw.

Once more she decided to rise. Once more she remained stiff and immobile. Her mouth felt unnaturally dry and no adequate sentences formed in her mind. She glanced back over her shoulder at the thirteen.

Milton sat rigidly beside Belda, as if he were a general about to face battle. Greg, so close to Cathy and the group of the girls in the back, was not, as he usually was, joking with them. Noa's eyes had skimmed past Cathy to Marie. She did not allow them to return to her niece.

For the first time since the tour had begun, Marie had relinquished her seat as chairman of the back of the bus to gaze distraughtly from a center window at the clusters of mud houses the exact color of the rolling terrain. In front of her, Moulay, his eyes firmly closed, was meditating. Had they all taken their mood of heaviness and gloom from Taber and her? Or was it simply that no one wanted to return to Fez?

Wendell had been in the dining room when she had gone down at six. He had started at once for Fez, was probably there by now. She envied his enjoying the comfort of the lush hotel scheduled for tonight's stay.

Eventually Johnny Ramos must have decided to extend his duty as bus driver and he became tour guide also. He reached for the microphone and started talking about olive trees and almond trees. He had just replaced the microphone when, hit by another rush of inspiration, he scooped it up again. "See up ahead," Johnny said, with his not-quite-correct English pronunciation. "A stork is nesting on the minaret."

As they drew closer, he pulled the bus to a stop so they could observe the high tower, see the stork's nest square in the center, with the bird immobile, as if waiting for them to take pictures. Only Belda complied, snapping a shot from the window.

All during the endless drive back to Fez, Johnny personally saw to it that the tour was not cheated out of precious information. For this Noa felt grateful and was glad she had not fired him.

They arrived in Fez later than had been scheduled. They settled themselves into the Atlas Hotel, very close to the battered old wall that separated the modern city from the old town.

Noa's theories now had to be proven. Noa wanted to lose no time going into the medina and checking the fountain for the rock used to beat up Wendell. It somehow seemed necessary that she get there before someone else did. By the time she had everyone checked into his room and had gone over the details of tomorrow's tour of the

Royal Palace, it had grown very late. The sky showed the first signs of darkness.

In the waning light, the three entrances to the gate of the medina looked even more like large keyholes. She crowded past several tourists, who bargained with a man whose arms were strung with bracelets of plated silver, and started following the medina wall. The dimness magnified its corrosion. The layer of stucco that remained was badly cracked and spattered with the dirt of ages. Ahead a decorative tower caught the last rays of sunlight and glimmered a silverish blue.

To quell her fears, Noa walked briskly and forced her eyes not to dwell on the gaping doorways and windows, especially not on the wide-open shops, grown obscure with shadows.

The path narrowed and seemed to become suddenly deserted, except for an old man in a soiled and torn robe, who emitted a mournful wail. The rising and falling of his voice did not sound like the chanting of Moulay on the bus, but it was no doubt a prayer. It grew higher and more pitiful as she caught up with him. Noa had started to slip around him before she noticed his cane and heard above his chanting the tap of it on the cobblestones.

Appalled by his raggedness and his blindness, she shrank against the wall as she passed him. She had started quickly away, when she felt drawn back by a rush of pity at his blind wanderings, the cruel harshness of his life. She stopped and dug into her red tour bag with the golden letters *Carlson-Rand Tours* for the few bills she had at the last minute decided to take along. She took a few reluctant steps back and gave him the money.

The volume of his wail increased, startling her. His white, unseeing eyes made her flinch. A talon hand reached out for her.

The thin, veined fingers of the grasping hand were exactly like the ones in her nightmares! Feeling like a little child again, she couldn't stop herself from running. Tall buildings on either side seemed to close in on her; the street became narrower. Had she tried she could have touched both sides of them.

Soon Noa reached the steps and below them the winding maze of paths. She had to be careful that she selected the one that led to the fountain. The thought of the open square, where light would still filter through, brightened her spirits.

Upon reaching the square, her eyes fell first to Ali Balsam's store, closed for the night, the huge doors solidly locked and barred. She hesitated, hearing the loud sound of splashing water in the surrounding quietness.

Nervously, she approached the fountain. Awkward fingers removed and replaced several of the loose stones until the sound of footsteps caused her to draw back.

A lone man wearing a shapeless gray jellaba entered the square. His head was bent, hood dropping forward, concealing his features. He was short and squat. This was not a form she recognized. She leaned over and pretended to be drinking, aware of the uneven sound of his step. The skirt of the jellaba dragged against the walkway as he moved by her.

The minute he was out of sight, Noa worked to ease the rock at the base of the column from its setting. Once in her hand she drew in her breath. Even in the dimming light, she could make out the darkish stain of Wendell's blood. She had been right! At least now she had in her possession the weapon. Was it covered with Cathy's fingerprints?

She handled the stone with great care, almost as if it were alive. She must be careful to preserve the fingerprints or any other evidence that the rock might reveal.

Footsteps again. She straightened up quickly and saw that it was only the blind beggar. She had nothing to fear from him.

Noa waited, listening to the uncertain clacking of his cane. He started to pass by her, but suddenly stopped, head tilted, blind eyes staring up into the darkening sky. He resumed his chanting, this time more of a pleading prayer to Allah. He knew she was there. Unseeing eyes tried to locate her. Noa made no motion, continued to hold the stone until he started to move on again, then she placed the rock into the tour bag she had brought along for the purpose.

As she straightened up again, her eye caught a glimpse of white from the empty hole where the stone had been set. She ran her hand into the opening, feeling the smoothness of cloth. Once the cloth was in her hand, she determined it was a simple white handkerchief, but something was wrapped inside it. She carefully unfolded it. Belda's emerald ring glowed against the white cloth!

Noa gasped. She hadn't expected ever to see this ring again. Her mind leaped for answers. Cathy must have been afraid of being caught with the jewel on her, so she had just stuffed the precious ring behind the rock she had then put back in the column of the fountain. Even though she was plotting to inherit a fortune upon Noa's death, Cathy still intended after the investigation had died down to return for this additional gain!

With shaking fingers Noa took the chain holding the Hand of Fatimah charm from around her neck and threaded the ring onto it. Even in the stifling heat, her fingers were icy cold, barely able to perform the task. She paused a moment to press the jewel tight against her skin and cover it by the folds of her blouse.

This accomplished, she lifted the bag and began walking in the direction of the gate. A figure stepped out into the pathway and blocked her way.

A cold, dead expression filled the enormous spaces of Cathy's eyes as she faced Noa. Noa gripped the bag tightly. She could not bring herself to move or speak.

Resentment — the girl had tried to kill her, had very nearly succeeded — mixed with a deep sadness, overcoming Noa's desire to strike out at her. Into her mind rose lines from Mike's letter: *Still, she's my little girl. I love her.* Perhaps for Mike she could. . . .

"I know exactly what you've been doing," Noa said in a level tone. "But I'm willing to forget it and let you go back to New York."

"I can't go back to New York!" Cathy's voice rose irrationally.

Intending to calm her, Noa took a step closer.

"You don't know anything!" Cathy yelled. She sprinted forward, knocking Noa aside, and began running to the right. She passed Ali Balsam's store and disappeared into the dark maze of small passageways.

Noa had prepared herself for an attack. She had certainly not expected the girl just to run away. Noa entered the square again, paused a moment beside the fountain to collect herself, then entered the alleyway. High buildings and blackened doorways, but no sign of Cathy.

She could be hiding anywhere, just waiting for Noa to enter. With hearing as alert as that of the blind man she had seen, Noa moved forward. "Cathy!"

The darkness was so thick Noa could not see the ground. She felt jolted by the uneven rocks beneath her feet. She should just go back. It would be so easy to become lost in these twisting walkways, just as she had been lost here when Taber had found her.

Noa made certain she kept a straight course. After what seemed like ages, she found herself facing a great, wooden gate that at night was used to close off part of the medina. Memories assailed her — the pain of her own small fists beating against very high doors, she as a child thinking that safety must surely lie just beyond the locked gates!

Her eyes skimmed the area she had just walked through. She must have passed Cathy concealed somewhere, in one of the arched doorways or behind some still-hanging displays. Noa started back the way she had come, eyes more accustomed now to the lack of light.

"Noa!"

Noa whirled back. From this distance Cathy seemed only a shadow, a shade darker than the gate behind her. Noa could not make out her features or the insanity, the hatred, that they must reveal.

"I thought you'd go back to the hotel," Cathy said.

Noa stepped closer to her. "I'm not trying to cheat you out of your inheritance. Mike knew I'd be fair with you. I want you to trust him and me."

She was close enough now to see Cathy's features. She was surprised by the emotion she read in them. Cathy was staring past her. Noa turned to see what it was that caused such fear. As she did, Cathy darted around her and bolted into the nearest alleyway.

Noa could hardly believe it! Cathy had run away again! No use following her this time, she decided, looking down the winding pathway. She would only get lost herself. She must return the way she had come while she still knew the direction of the fountain.

Noa's feet falling against the rocks seemed to echo in the great stillness. Or was someone walking behind her? What game was Cathy playing? Was she trying to wear her down, attack Noa when she least expected it?

She stopped and her eyes strained for some movement. When she detected none, she started on again. In her haste the tour bag banged against a stand where old brass pots were stacked. They clanged together as they struck the ground.

The walk back seemed much longer, the steps up and down more laborious. At last she saw the square, lit by a single bulb gleaming dimly above the fountain.

Noa stopped for a moment beside the fountain to catch her breath. Not much further now back to the hotel!

Footsteps, steady and heavy, were coming from the path she had just left. Cathy, like last time, must have followed her. Noa dropped the tour bag and prepared herself for whatever was to come.

The form that appeared wore a dark jellaba, but the hood was tossed back and revealed his face to her.

Greg did not look like a boyish college student from New Jersey, but then, of course, he wasn't. His features, viewed by the lone light above the fountain, were singularly cruel. The narrowed eyes reflected the glint from the bulb as he said, "I'll take the ring."

Noa made no movement. Why hadn't she realized it? Greg was Cathy's boyfriend — the evil influence Mike had spoken of in his letter! His deciding to take the tour too was the reason Cathy had changed her mind about coming along. He was the boyfriend Cathy kept meeting, not Johnny Ramos, not Taber! With Noa dead, they would have Mike's fortune for themselves. How clever of Greg to set up the series of robberies so that when she was killed, only an impersonal thief would be suspected!

"The ring," he said. "Or do you want me to rip it off your neck?"

Noa glanced down at the bag. If she could lift the rock before he was able to reach her, she could use it as a weapon against him.

As Greg stepped slowly forward, his hand

slipped inside the jellaba. "A little souvenir of Morocco I purchased this evening." He unsheathed a dagger, hurling the brass-plated cover far away from him. It made a thud as it hit the ground. The twisted end of the blade caught the light overhead.

Noa grabbed for the rock, sprang forward, and hit him as hard as she could. The blow, landing on the side of his head, did not faze him. He grabbed her arm. The rock slipped from her grasp.

Greg's steellike fingers tightened on her wrist. She could not break free.

The hand that held the dagger jerked backward, preparing to thrust the cruel blade into the space below her ribs.

Noa expected to feel an explosion of pain, then blood flowing from her body. Instead, she saw the blade of the knife being drawn suddenly upward.

Taber hurled Greg backward. Greg fell and turned, and his fingers clawed at the rocks as he tried to rise. Taber dived forward, a hand snaked around Greg's neck.

Both men rose simultaneously. She could see Taber's clenched lips. His fist slammed against Greg's jaw, pounded his stomach. Greg, with a moan, fell again. This time he did not move.

Taber wiped his face with a bleeding

hand. It left a trail of blood across his jaw. "Cathy came after me," he said with a quick intake of breath. "She said you had started back toward the fountain."

"Why would she want to help me?" Noa's words stopped short. "You mean she didn't know about the robberies or about any of this?"

"Cathy knew no more than we did. She thought Greg was just going on the tour so they could be together. She had no idea what his real motive was until you were nearly killed in Casablanca."

"Cathy saw him tonight in the medina," Noa said. "That's why she ran away to get you."

Taber reached for her. Noa leaned her head against his shoulder. Her fear of death and her terror of the dark medina surfaced again with such force that it caused a sudden spell of shaking. Taber gathered her close.

"Darling," he said, "don't cry now. It's all over!"

Chapter Thirteen

Belda's ring glittered upon her finger as she stopped to hug Noa. "Thank you for getting my ring back! I thought it was lost forever. I guess everything turned out for the best, after all. It's too bad about Greg, though. He seemed like such a nice young man."

"Belda's always been one to be fooled by a pretty face," Milton said with a wink. His good humor had reappeared with the return of Belda's ring. "That's why she needs me to look after her. Come on, old gal. We don't want to keep our ride waiting."

"We'll keep in touch, Noa, I told Miltie this morning that I'm booking your next Spanish tour. We won't go, though, unless you're the guide!"

"I'll never give up being a guide. I'll be looking forward to our next trip!" As they disappeared out the glass lobby doors of the Hotel Tangier, Noa realized how much she would miss them.

Moulay Aziz approached and offered Noa his hand. "I, too, will book another of your tours."

"I hope so. Good-bye, Moulay."

Suitcase in hand, Moulay left for the train station. Noa watched him, wondering which of his two wives he would go home to first.

"See? Thirteen isn't such an unlucky number, after all," Taber said.

Noa turned to face his charming smile. "Except for Greg. What will happen to him?"

"Because he's an American citizen, he'll probably be extradited back to the States. But he'll still face charges of theft and attempted murder."

"I'm just so grateful that Cathy had nothing to do with it! Greg never lived in New Jersey; he lived right next to Mike and Cathy in New York. He's the one who stole Mike's coin collection and the other things from the condo. Greg was the bad influence Mike warned me about in his letter."

"And Greg was the one Cathy was sneaking out to meet, not Johnny — or me," Taber said, smiling. "In Casablanca, when I didn't go on the tour, it was because Cathy was so afraid. She confided a lot of things to me that day, but nothing I could prove."

After a while, Taber continued, "At first,

Cathy thought Greg had booked the tour so that they could be together. She thought it was great fun pretending not to know him, sharing his secret. It was all a big game to her until the thefts and accidents began to happen. Then Cathy began to suspect what Greg was really up to. She finally realized how far he was willing to go and she turned to me, thinking I could save you."

Noa shivered a little. "Greg planned to murder me and marry Cathy so that he could have Mike's inheritance." Noa thought of the afternoon when he had proposed to her at Rick's Café. His words had been as phony and insincere as the atmosphere of the place had been. If she had said yes, it would have saved him the trouble of killing her. He intended to get his hands on Mike's money any way he could — by marrying her, or by killing her and marrying Cathy. When she turned him down, he tried to stage her accidental death by running her down in the mysterious car.

Marie stepped out of the elevator. Noa wondered how she could ever have felt anything but admiration for her, for her alertness, for her air of command. "Come on," Marie said to them. "Wendell is waiting for us in the coffee shop."

She led the way, saying over her shoulder,

"You're not going to believe this, but Cathy and I had a long talk. She wants to spend her senior year in boarding school so she can be with Orva. I think it's a good idea. The girl does have potential."

Wendell walked forward to join them. "Marie and I plan to marry July fifteenth," he announced, putting his arm around her. "That's really why I've been looking around for a reliable partner." He smiled. "Marie's a tyrant. She's going to insist I give up some of the work load."

"Married?" Noa's surprise mixed with joy. "I'm so happy for you!"

"Yes, a lot of changes. You and I, business partners." Wendell gave a short laugh. "If I were smart, I'd have chosen Taber Rand. Changing the name of the company to Carlson-Parker is going to cost me a small fortune." His large eyes widened in mock exasperation. "Think of it, Taber. New letterhead, paint jobs for all the vans. . . ."

"Stop right there, Wendell. Noa and I have thought up a way to save you a lot of trouble and expense."

"It doesn't seem right, changing the company name after so long," Noa explained. "So I've decided to change my name instead."

Wendell's eyes grew even wider as he

239

stared at the two of them. "Does this mean what I think it means?"

"It means that Noa and I are getting married!" Ignoring Wendell's expression and Marie's astonishment, Taber pulled Noa close and kissed her. "Wendell Carlson, meet your new partner — Noa Rand."